Things Every Good Woman Should Know

Volume 1

Jae Henderson

Things Every Good Woman Should Know: Volume 1

Copyright © 2014 by Jean Henderson

Printed in the United States

Put It In Writing
735 North Parkway
Memphis, TN 38105

This book is dedicated to my mother, Lillie Marshall, and my grandmother, Mae Marshall. They are no longer on this earth but their presence is always felt. The sage advice of these two women continues to guide me. Thank you for showing me in word and deed what being a good woman means. I love you and miss you madly.

TABLE OF CONTENTS

X

ACKNOWLEDGMENTS

This is my fourth book and my first book of short stories. I pray that it is accepted well. I appreciate everyone who has helped to make this possible. A special thank you to my editor, Alanna Boutin. You help keep me from making the same mistakes repeatedly. Thank you to my friends Tracy Robinson, Rachelle Butler and my cousin Faith Marshall for you honest critiques and assistance. To the rest of my family, I love you and I appreciate your loving and supporting me in return. To my church family, Olivet Fellowship Baptist Church and my pastor, Dr. Eugene Gibson, Jr., it is your spiritual nourishment and real-life applicable teachings that help make me equipped to do the same through my writing. Thank you to my readers and the book clubs who have given me their support and feedback. Please keep it coming. You help make me a better author. Thank you to all the people on my publicity team. Let's take this one worldwide! Last, but certainly not least, thank you to my Heavenly Father from who all blessings flow. I am humbled, grateful, and honored that you chose me to be a vessel for your word.

FOREWORD

I'm sure that you are asking yourself as I once did, "What is a good woman?" The answer is sure to elicit several different answers, each from the unique perspective of the giver. Yet, one cannot argue that there are certain attributes that most certainly accompany the words "good woman". The simplest definition I have found is a woman after God's own heart; a woman who tries to live according to God's word, not only for the benefit of herself but those around her. Being good doesn't mean being perfect. None of us can get it right all the time. It merely means that we try, and when we lose our way, we are open to correction.

The *I'm a Good Woman* series is my attempt to offer some advice before one of my sisters veers off the positive path. I've learned through trial and error that, more often than not, life is simpler and more peaceful when we do the right thing. Wisdom definitely comes with age, and the mistakes I made in my youthful folly have impacted the years that followed. Each one of my stories is accompanied by what I call moral messaging or a lesson learned. I hope you enjoy the lessons each of my characters learn, but better yet, I hope something that is said impacts your life in a positive way. Love yourself enough to do the right thing.

You Are Beautiful

God has made everything beautiful in its own time. He has plant-ed eternity in the human heart, but even so, people cannot see the whole scope of God's work from beginning to end—Ecclesiastes 3:11

It's funny how people can be closely related and look almost noth-ing alike. I have two sisters. All three of us are attractive, but we have virtually no physical similarities. My oldest sister, Vanessa, is 26. She has been what brothers label as "thick" her entire life. She's got "Proud Mary" thighs, childbearing hips, an out-to-there derrière, and voluptuous breasts. Her curves were always her ticket to getting almost anything she wanted from a man. Now, after two kids and a failed marriage, all Vanessa does is complain about how fat she is and how she wishes she could lose weight and make more money. Let's not forget about her no-good, trifling baby daddy, Darryl. She's basically raising her and Darryl's two children, who are now ages 7 and 9, on her own. Darryl sends sporadic child support checks and spends time with them occasionally; but that's all he does.

Now, my middle sister, Tasha, is 5 feet tall and 98 pounds soaking wet. She's also 24, but looks like she's in junior high. She's as cute as a button, but hates that she is so little. I guess at some point I would get tired of high school boys hitting on me too. She and her built-like-a-linebacker boyfriend, Reggie, make an odd couple, but he loves him some Tasha and spoils her rotten.

They are currently engaged but haven't set a date for the wedding. Tasha wants both of her sisters as her maids of honor, but our unhap-py older sister says there's no way Tasha's putting her on display in some dress she's sure will be ugly. That's Vanessa. Even on our sister's wedding day, it's got to be about her.

I'm extremely proud of Tasha, and I will be there right by her side, beaming with pride. Tasha is also an entrepreneur. She has a fashion boutique that caters specifically to petite women, like herself. It's called The Perfect Fit, and nothing in her store is above a size 7. I am 5 foot 9, so I can't wear a thing in there but the shirts. I tried on a suit once, and the arms of the jacket stopped before they reached my wrists. The pants looked like ankle beaters!

Then there's me, Dawn. I'm the youngest of the Williams sisters. Now, the only thing thick about me is my skin. As a kid, I was crackhead-thin. The kids at my school teased me unmercifully. I was called "Olive Oyl," "crack baby," and "Somalia kid." I hated those commercials asking people to donate to children suffering from poverty and malnourishment in Somalia. People would come to school the next day and say, "I saw you on TV again."

I was tall with no breasts, no hips, and no booty, so people could not believe that "brick-house" Vanessa or "too cute" Tasha were my sisters. It became common for me to hear things like, "You're so skinny you could hula-hoop with a Cheerio," or "When you step on the scale, a note comes on that reads, *Are you on yet*??" As a result, I developed thick skin real fast.

As I got older, I gained a little weight and started to fill out some. I now have small breasts, small hips, and a small round peach-shaped booty. I look good in a pair of jeans, if I do say so myself. I'm also a size 6, and people are always asking me if I model. I still think my body could use a little improvement here and there, but whose couldn't? I'd be lying if I said I didn't still have some hang-ups from all those years of being teased as a child. Other people keep telling me I look good, so I take their word for it, coordinate my outfits the best that I can, and thank God for every day I breathe. I'm still a proud card-carrying member of the A Cup Club, but I don't mind; and the men in my life don't seem to mind either. I remember in high school, my best friend Tyra and I developed a motto: "*All a brother needs is a mouthful,*" and I got that covered.

I am currently in a relationship with a wonderful musician named Tyler. He plays bass in a band called Trifecta; it consists of him and his two cousins, Mike and L-Ray. They perform at several clubs around town, and they're working on their first album. I'm a local R&B singer, but not for long. Last month, I signed with Yum Yum Records, and before long, Dawn Williams will be a household name. Tomorrow I'm going on my first photo shoot for the label. I can't wait, but first, I have to get some sleep. I want to be well rested for tomorrow.

My alarm chimed at 5 a.m. I drowsily hit the snooze button. *Just 15 more minutes,* I thought to myself. *They told me to come as I am, so I don't really have to get up and get glamorous.* I lay there yearning for more rest, but then I felt Tyler pat me on my stomach.

"Get up, Pussycat," he said. "You don't want to be late for your first shoot. You have to be there at six, right?"

I love when he calls me Pussycat, but I made him promise to only do it in private. He told me my body was sleek and sexy like a cat. I always thought the term *sleek* was best used when describing cars, but it turns him on, and that's all that matters. I fought my body's lack of desire to move, pulled myself out of bed, and headed to the bathroom. I'm sure "come as you are" doesn't include not bathing or brushing my teeth.

In 20 minutes I was ready and headed out the door. I decided to wear my favorite velour jogging suit, a sports bra, and a brand-new pair of Jordans. These shoes are expensive, but I loved Michael Jordan as a teen. He was talented and fine! All the guys in my school talked about was how they wanted to be like Mike. All of us girls wanted to be his girlfriend, even though he was still married to his first wife, Juanita.

The shoot was in a warehouse that didn't look like much of anything on the outside, but on the inside, it was a top-notch studio called Picture Perfect. All the high-end photographers used it because the owner's design team was able to create the perfect set for any shoot. Once, they even turned one of their rooms into a beach, complete with sand, water, and palm trees. Of course, their "make-your-dreams-come-true" services are not cheap, but when you're dealing with companies with million-dollar budgets, who cares? When I got there, I was met at the door by my manager, Melvin, and the wardrobe stylist Gabriella.

Gabriella took one look at me and said, "Darling, you are lovely. I see you've had your nails done, so that is one thing we won't worry about. We're going to have fun together, and when I get through with you, you won't even recognize yourself."

"Great," I said, as she grabbed my hand and whisked me away to get my hair done. She introduced me to the hairstylist, Dontae. I'd heard he's fabulous. He's done hair for the best of them: Halle Berry, Mary J. Blige, and the late great Whitney Houston. It was obvious he's sweeter than sugarcane, and you could tell he was proud of it.

"Girlfriend," he said, smacking his extremely glossy lips, "I'm gonna make you look like the star you are destined to be." He snapped a *before* picture, and then said, "Follow me to the shampoo bowl, baby, so I can hook you up."

After washing and conditioning my hair, Dontae decided to do a sew-in weave to lengthen and thicken my strands. My hair is short and a little on the thin side; it's something I inherited from my mother. It also doesn't have any weight to it, so it never stays in place. Any way the wind blows, it goes. I usually wear a short pixy cut. It's chic, functional, and best of all, low maintenance. Dontae got to work, and in about 3 hours, my now platinum streaked brown hair was past my shoulders, flat-ironed straight, and runway gorgeous.

"You look fierce, girlfriend. Fierce. A star is born, courtesy of Hair Designs by Dontae. You gotta man, Lady Bug?" Dontae asked.

"Yes," I replied.

"He's going to be all over you when you get home. Now, don't let him pull your tracks out. This is that Grade-A Malaysian hair, honey. If you take care of it, it will take care of you and last at least 2 months or more. Now, you get out of here and go see Miss Missy in makeup."

"Thank you, Dontae," I said. "I love it."

"You're welcome, sweetheart. I'll get your *after* photo when you're finished getting all dolled up. Up high, girlfriend." I raised my hand and slapped him a high five.

Missy was one of those middle-aged white chicks who has watched way too much BET. She was wearing a huge blond Afro with brown highlights. The name Michael was tattooed on her left arm in cursive letters. I wondered if that was her baby's daddy. She also had DIVA tattooed on the right side of her neck. Her Apple Bottom jeans weren't working in her favor, because her booty still looked as flat as a park bench. Although baby may not have had back, she had plenty of front. Her fitted top hung low to reveal her surgically enhanced breasts. The left one was adorned with another tattoo that read "Missy" and had a pair of red lips beneath it.

"Hey, Boo," she squealed. "That hair is tiiiight. Now, it's time to put on your makeup." She gasped. "Sweet baby Jesus lying in a manger! When's the last time you arched your eyebrows?" she asked as she peered at me with her nose less than 2 inches away from my face. Her breath smelled like Big Red chewing gum. She put her hand under my chin and turned my head from side to side. "Tsk, tsk, tsk! You have got to do better. You got two caterpillars on your face," she chided.

"I don't know. You're welcome to hook me up, but do me a favor. Don't shave them off and draw me some more. I can't stand that. Plus, I don't think I could draw them myself. I know I couldn't do each one the same. So, after today, I'd be walking around looking crazy if you shaved them," I said.

"I can work wit' whatcha got, boo. We gon' put you on some lashes, too. Now sit in my chair and let's get crack-a-lackin'.'"

When's the last time I heard someone say that word? The '90s?

After about 40 minutes, Missy finished and handed me a mirror. I screamed, "Aaaaaah, I look beautiful! You made me beautiful. Thank you!" I threw my arms around her neck and almost knocked her off her feet.

"Baby boo, didn't anybody tell you that you were already beauti-ful? With those great big ole baby browns and that smooth caramel skin, it wasn't hard to get you looking fine as a bottle of Merlot. Now, take yo' sexy self to wardrobe before I kiss you dead in da mouf, and I don't even like women," she laughed.

I scurried out of her chair, and she patted me on my booty. "You go, girl!" she said and snapped her fingers.

I was so happy about my hair and makeup that I barely even no-ticed Gabriella waiting for me next to several racks of clothes. I almost bumped into her trying to get to the huge mirror in wardrobe so I could look at myself again.

"Careful darling," she said. "Let's see what we have here." She looked me up and down from head to toe without saying a word. Then she picked out my first outfit which consisted of a pair of skintight jeans, a sick blue sleeveless shirt with a plunging V-neckline made of suede and leather, and blue stilettos. After, I tried on everything she looked at me again and shook her head.

"The jeans look good on you, but the shirt I'm not sure about. You don't have much breasts, so it doesn't hang right. Let me see if I can push them up a bit." Her thick Italian accent seemed to emphasize each word, which made them seem extra insulting. She had me try on several push-up bras, drop-in titties, and she event wrapped me in duct tape. I felt like I was being molested the way Gabriella's cold hands moved around my breasts touching an adjusting them in an effort to give them some lift.

Eventually, she let out a huge sigh and said, "This isn't working. You'll have to wear a different top."

I'd always known I had small breasts, but she made it seem like it was some type of deformity.

"In this business, bigger is better; so you may want to look into implants in the near future. Put this on," she said while handing me a plain white T-shirt with "Rock This" on the front in black letters. When I came from behind the dressing curtain, she dropped the rubber titties down my shirt, and positioned them correctly. When she dropped those boobs on me, I swear I felt my self-esteem plummet to the floor. I know I don't have much, but the shirt she originally had me try on made this one look like garbage. She put some dangling earrings in my ears and slid four large metallic bangles on my left arm. At least my Giuseppe Zanotti shoes were cute.

Gabriella looked me up and down again. "This will have to do. Off to the set you go." *What happened to we're going to have fun? This feels like a root canal.*

Melvin was waiting for me on the set. He has headed my career for the past 3 years. He and I have pretty good chemistry; but what I love most about him is he sees my vision, and he believes in me. He truly believes I'm going to be a star, and he's working just as hard as I am to get me there. He immediately noticed that something was wrong and pulled me to the side.

"You look great, Dawn, but you don't look happy. What's wrong?"

I tried to tell him what happened while holding back the tears. I couldn't cry because if I did, I'd mess up my makeup. I relayed my story as quickly as possible without shedding a single tear.

"Dawn, the entertainment industry is about perception and illusion. We give the public what we want them to see. If implants is what it takes for you to gain fans and make millions, then do it. This is your dream. Don't ruin it because you have a problem with a little nip and tuck here and there. You look fabulous. Your pictures are going to turn out fabulous. After the shoot, we'll talk to the people in artist development and see if this is the direction they're trying to go. If you need a better rack, we'll get it for you, babe. It's no big deal. I got you."

I was in such shock that all I could say was, "Okay." I thought Melvin would take my side and tell Gabriella to leave me alone, shut up, do her job, and be happy about it.

"You look real good, babe. Don't fight it." He kissed me on the cheek, smiled, turned me in the direction of the photographer, and gently pushed me forward. I was dismissed.

Now, the photographer was this superfine brother named Jermaine. He's from England and speaks with this great accent. Every time he opened his mouth, I could've sworn he was channeling Idris Elba. I'd seen his work in hundreds of magazines, and he could make a corpse look sexy. He took one look at me and yelled for Gabriella. She came skipping over. He looked at her and said, "With boobs like these, why isn't she showing them off? I need cleavage. You know I like the ta-tas in my shots."

Gabriella snickered. "Jermaine, darling, those are not hers. They are courtesy of me and my portable Tupperware set."

They both laughed as I cringed with embarrassment but remained silent.

"Can't you do something? I want to see some skin. She's a new artist, and I want her pictures to ooze sexiness. They need to scream every man's fantasy and every woman's muse."

"Afraid not," Gabriella answered. "The only thing she's got is nipples, and you can't show those in magazines. You're gonna have to Photoshop this one."

By this time, my eyes were welling up with tears again. They were talking about me as if I wasn't standing right there. Jermaine noticed me straining to hold back the tears and said, "I'm sorry. You're sensitive about your flat chest. I apologize. Don't cry. Let's get to work. You are such a pretty girl. Don't make such a sad face. Jermaine will make you look like the rock star written across the place where your bosom is supposed to be. Now smile." I did as I was told. His camera flashed.

After 4 hours and 4 additional clothing, hair, and makeup changes, complete with rubber titties, we were finished with the photo shoot. I was exhausted, my cheeks hurt from smiling, and all I wanted to do was go home and lie down. Jermaine was very nice the remainder of the shoot, but he kept telling me to stick my chest out. His initial insults stuck in my mind the entire time. But I had a job to do, so I plastered a fake smile on my face and did it. I had to show Yum Yum Records I had the right image and work ethic to go along with my talent. After all, this was my big break.

On my way out the door, Melvin grabbed me and said, "You handled that like a pro. I took the liberty of getting the name and number of Missy's plastic surgeon. Give him a call and make an appointment for a consultation. You really do look better with bigger boobs, babe."

I mumbled thanks and headed to the dressing area to take off my clothes. Gabriella was there packing up.

"Melvin told me you might be considering implants. Keep the falsies and try them out for a few days before you make a decision. Although, I'm sure you'll get the implants. It's a wonder you hadn't done it before now."

Who asked her for her opinion?

I undressed in silence, put my jogging suit on, and threw the falsies in my bag. I had to get out of there. My self-esteem was dragging on the floor, and it took every ounce of self-control I had not to scream. I was hoping that nobody else would step on it before I could make it home. If someone did, I may have hit a note so high that it would've shattered the sound barrier. What a difference a few hours could make. I was so happy when I got there, but by the time I left, I was wishing I had never come. Is that what stardom is like? People thinking they have the right to constantly criticize you because you don't look the way they think you should?

I drove my convertible Volkswagen Beetle home with the radio off. I usually listened to songs from my upcoming album when in the car. They were pretty good if I say so myself. Others have told me it's going to be a hit, but at that moment, that didn't matter. I'd been told by three people in one day that I was physically unattractive. I couldn't wait to get home and cuddle up in the arms of my man. Tyler always had a way of making me feel better.

Unfortunately, the house was empty, except for our cat, Tabitha. Tyler was probably still at the studio. I made myself a salad with grilled chicken breast and doused it with low-fat ranch dressing. I'd barely eaten two bites when I put down my fork. I hadn't eaten all day, but I wasn't hungry. I decided to go to my room and lie down. Maybe I'd feel better after a nap. I looked in the mirror at my stellar makeup job. I wished I had skills like Missy; I would look like a rock star every day.

I unzipped my jogging suit jacket, removed my sports bra, and stood in the mirror looking at myself. No, I'll never be a DD, but I honestly thought I looked okay. I'm a small woman, with small breasts. That makes me evenly proportioned, right? I wrapped my weave around my head, tied it up in a silk scarf, and put on a shower cap. Then I stepped into the shower, turned the water on, and let the tears flow. In a matter of seconds, the water and tears washed away my flawless makeup.

How can people be so mean? I'd been nice to everybody today. I didn't deserve that treatment.

After about 10 minutes of crying, I heard somebody enter the bathroom. The shower curtain slid back, and there was the love of my life standing in front of me buck-naked in all of his glorious manhood. My man is blessed, and I love every inch of him; from his low-cut hair to his badly in need of a pedicure feet. Tyler is everything I ever wanted in a man. He's 6 foot 5 with shiny, smooth, dark skin that reminds me of a moonlit night, strong arms, and a perfectly sculpted chest that he works hard to maintain by going to the gym at least 4 days a week. His lips look more luscious than fresh-picked cherries. He's got silky smooth hands, and he knows exactly what to do with them. He's talented in other ways, too. As I mentioned before, he plays bass guitar, and whenever I go to his shows, I see all the women in the audience look at him with lustful eyes, but I just smile and think to myself, *I'm the one he comes home to every night. All you can do is dream when I experience delicious reality repeatedly.*

We've been together 2 years, and we're both full-time struggling artists. We don't have much money, which is why we moved in together against both our parents' wishes. They believe a couple should be married before they live together. I get so tired of hearing how we are living in sin and God isn't pleased. Cohabitating seems so much more practical. God knows we're broke. We were always at each other's place anyway. It didn't make sense for us to both pay rent. We've been living together about 6 months now, and so far so good. I often dream of us getting married and being one of Hollywood's powerful couples like Will and Jada Smith, Tim McGraw and Shania Twain, or Jay-Z and Beyoncé. It's coming. I can feel it, but we've both gotta keep working hard and dreaming big.

When he stepped in the shower, I tried to turn my head so he wouldn't notice my red eyes, but It didn't work. He cupped my face in his hands and looked at me quizzically.

"What's wrong, Pussycat?" There was genuine concern in his eyes.

I tried to answer, but the only thing that came out was a loud wail and more tears. Tyler turned off the shower, wrapped me in a towel, and led me into our bedroom. He told me to sit on the bed and asked his question again. I still couldn't speak, so he started asking me more questions.

"Did somebody die?"

I shook my head no.

"Are you injured?"

I shook my head no again.

"Can I make it better?"

I nodded my head up and down. "Just hold me," I whimpered.

He said, "I'll do you one better," and began to kiss me slowly. His delicious kisses traveled from my cheek to my lips and worked their way down to my neck. His skin was still moist from the shower, but I didn't mind. He pressed his luscious lips against my body, never allowing each kiss to linger in the same spot too long. When he got to my breasts, the memories from earlier that day came flooding back, and I made him stop. He gave me a puzzled look.

"What do you think of my body?" I asked.

"I love your body, and if you hadn't interrupted me, I was about to show you how much."

"This is important, Tyler. What do you think of my breasts?"

"Baby, I love all of you."

He was avoiding the question, and I knew it. "That's not what I asked you, Tyler."

"Pussycat, I would tell you the truth, but I don't think you can handle it."

"I need to hear it. Today at the shoot, three people suggested that I get breast implants. Now, tell me what you think of them."

"First, tell me what happened," he said. I knew he was stalling for time, but I needed an answer and I wasn't going to give him a reason not to give me one. I sat in his lap, and he wrapped his strong, muscular arms around me while I gave him the condensed version of the day's events.

When I finished, Tyler looked at me and said, "Rough day, huh? If you really want to know, the first time I saw you naked I was a little disappointed. You do have small breasts, but it doesn't bother me anymore because you have other attributes. Your face is beautiful, and your hips and booty should be the prototype for all women. You have a great personality, and you make me extremely happy. I feel so good when I'm with you. I feel like with you by my side I can accomplish anything."

I couldn't believe what I'd heard. I removed his hands from my body and stood up. "So, you think I should get implants, too?" I asked in shock.

"No, I didn't say that. What I'm saying is that they could be bigger, but it's not something I dwell on. I wouldn't mind if you got implants, but I've already accepted the way you look, and I've resolved to live with it. If the label thinks getting implants will help your career, it might not be such a bad idea. Give it some thought. Now, may I finish making love to my woman?"

He pulled me close and began kissing me again, but the moment had been ruined for me. I wriggled away from him and headed to the dresser to get my pajamas.

Tyler sat on the bed in disbelief, like I was doing something wrong. I put them on and got in the bed. It was only 4 p.m., but I was tired. Tyler lay next to me, let out a deep breath, and stared at the ceiling. He let out another deep breath and asked, "What did I do wrong?"

"I needed you to tell me you thought I was beautiful just the way I am. That there's nothing wrong with me and not to change a thing. You have no idea what you did, do you?" I asked with hurt in my voice.

"No, what did I do besides give you an honest answer that you asked me to give?"

"You made me feel uglier than any of those people at the photo shoot. My man, who I thought believed I was gorgeous, has told me that I could be gorgeous if I had bigger breasts. I can't believe you told me you were disappointed the first time we made love. You know I'm self-conscious! You remember how when we first started sleeping together I would always go in the closet to change my clothes. As time went on, I stopped because I thought you thought I was hot. Now, I find out you think I'm flawed. Thanks a lot, Tyler! Well, guess what? You're not perfect either. Your head is shaped funny, your hands are too big for your body, and Mr. Always-At-Attention hooks to the right; but I never once thought that you were deformed because of it. I thought it made you unique!" I started to cry all over again.

"I told you, you couldn't handle the truth!" yelled Tyler. "Women!" he huffed as he rose from the bed. "I'm going downstairs!"

I stared at his naked body while he retrieved a pair of basketball shorts from the floor, where he'd left them this morning. "AND my penis does not hook to the right. That's your cocked eye looking in the wrong direction!" he snapped as he pulled the drawstring tight. I rolled onto my side with my back facing him.

"I am not cock-eyed!" I yelled and pounded my pillow in an effort to get comfortable. I then wrapped my arms tightly around myself to show myself some love, because it seemed no one else in the house was going to. I tried to go to sleep but I couldn't. I was too hurt to rest peacefully. I tossed and turned for hours until Tyler climbed in bed with me. He positioned his body close to mine and pushed his crotch into the back of my thigh.

"Baby, you asleep?" he asked. I acted like I didn't hear him. I wasn't in the mood to talk, and there was no way he was getting off the hook that night. He had to suffer. When I didn't answer he turned his body away from me and a few minutes later I heard the rhythmic breathing of his slumber. Even though I was upset with Tyler having his warm body near me brought some comfort and I found myself falling asleep too. I woke up when I heard Tyler getting ready to leave early the next morning. I continued to pretend that I was asleep when he rose, so he wouldn't try to talk to me again.

I got up a couple of hours later to go to breakfast with my father. I'm a daddy's girl to my very core, and my father and I get together as often as we can. That day, we met at IHOP for breakfast. He loves their pancakes with strawberries, whipped cream, and hot syrup. I love the waffles with the same fixings. When I arrived, he was standing by the front register waiting for me.

He greeted me with, "Hey, Pumpkin," and gave me a warm hug. My father is another man who could always see right through me. The puffy eyes I had from crying the night before probably didn't help with trying to hide my feelings either.

"What did that boy do? I told you not to live with a man that isn't your husband. All you young people want to do is screw and shack. Stop all this living in sin. I'll kill him if he put his hands on you!"

"Calm down, Daddy," I said. "The only thing Tyler has hurt is my feelings. Let's order our food, and then I'll tell you what happened."

The hostess showed us to our booth, and less than a minute later, our waitress came over to the table to take our order. Ordinarily, I probably wouldn't have noticed, but due to my current crisis, I zoned in on her huge breasts. She was probably about an EE cup, and she had three buttons undone on her blouse to expose her ample cleavage. *I thought this was IHOP, not Hooters.*

My retired, 65-year-old father talked to her without looking at her face. If the space between her breasts were a pool, he would have dove his geriatric behind in headfirst and probably drowned in utter bliss. I watched him as he fixated his gaze on her body; the waitress smiled, giggled, flirted, and batted her eyelashes as if she was enjoying the attention. My mom died of breast cancer 3 years ago, so I know my father gets lonely; but the way he was fawning over that woman was ridiculous. He was acting like he'd just hit puberty. I was thoroughly disgusted by the juvenile display of both parties involved. Although, I'm sure she was behaving that way in hopes of getting a big tip. I had a tip for her: *stop pimping yourself out for a couple of dollars!* I couldn't wait to finish giving her our orders so she would go away. As she walked off, my father took a quick look at her behind. Then, he turned back to me and said, "Now, what's the problem, Pumpkin?"

"*That's* my problem," I said and nodded in the direction of the waitress.

"The waitress? Do you know her?"

"No, but I know her breasts; and they're making small-chested women like me the target of disdain and ridicule."

I told him about the prior day's events, but left out the parts about me being naked in the shower with Tyler. I'm still Daddy's little girl, and some things Daddy doesn't need to know.

"Daddy, I don't get it. People holla all day about keeping it real and being transparent in everything but appearance. It seems like then, the faker the better. It's okay to be a walking Barbie doll; but tell a lie and the world will nail you to the wall. I have nothing against the enhancements. If people want to spend their money on fake boobs and booties, a new nose, Botox, false eyelashes, acrylic nails, contacts and some Indian woman's hair that flows down their back or whatever, that's cool. It's their money; but for those of us who are happy with however little or much God gave us, the world seems to say there's something wrong with us. Why, Daddy?" I asked.

"Well, Pumpkin," he began, "It's a fact of life that you don't have big breasts. It's also a fact of life that sex sells in the entertainment industry. Look at any music video or magazine, and all you'll see is some woman's assets sprawled on the cover and throughout the pages. Does that make it right? No, but it's a fact. Whether you change your appearance to conform to what's popular is up to you.

"You don't know this, but when you were in high school and it looked like you weren't going to develop, I mentioned it to your mother. I told her maybe we should take you to the doctor and get you checked out. She told me I would do no such thing. Her daughter was perfect the way she was, and not having big breasts wasn't the same as having an extra limb or 3 eyes; and if I didn't like you just the way you were, I could stop looking at you. Well, that was pretty much the end of that discussion. You were a late bloomer, and in time you did develop some.

"Don't tell your sisters, but I always thought you were the most attractive of all my girls. That might be because you look the most like your mother. Pumpkin, there's nothing wrong with you. But if you decide to get breast implants, you have to look at this thing from all sides. Any kind of surgery can be dangerous. There may be some serious side effects that can't be undone, and truthfully, sometimes the surgeon messes up. I read somewhere about a lady whose nipples were in the wrong place after surgery, and another whose breasts ended up hard and uneven. However, there are also women who are very happy with the results and experienced no negative side effects.

"Now, if you decide you want to do it, I still got all that money in the bank for college you decided not to use. I'll pay for it if you want, but make sure you're doing it for Dawn. Not for your manager, your stylist, or your man; because you're the one who will have to walk around with silicon or saline, or whatever they're making them air bags out of these days, in your chest."

I sat and listened attentively. Our food arrived and I hungrily began eating my waffle. Dad did the same. I knew my father meant well, but he didn't make me feel much better either. All I got out of that conversation was my father thought I was deformed too. So deformed, that at one point, he felt it was necessary to address my mother about it. I missed my momma. He did say I was prettier than my sisters, though. I liked that. I always thought Tasha was the prettiest.

As we finished our breakfast, he stopped and said, "You know your mother almost lost a breast to cancer. When she told me she was going have to cut one of them off, I didn't care. I wasn't concerned about how she would look naked with only one. The only thing I was concerned with was whether that surgery would keep my Martha here with me a little while longer. But when the doctors got in there, they realized that it wasn't only in her breast, but in her lungs too; and there was too much of it to remove."

I sat there with a bewildered look on my face. "I know you and your sisters didn't know that, but that's because your mother didn't want you to know. When she found out she had to have a mastectomy, she made me promise not to tell you. She was going to tell you after the surgery; but the surgery wasn't completed, and within a few months, the love of my life was gone. If that boyfriend of yours is so hung up on appearances that he can't see what a winner he's got, then tell him to pack his bags. Ask any man who's in a happy marriage to make a list of all the things that made him decide to make his wife the one, the mother of his children and the person he wants to grow old with. I bet you her breasts would be one of the last things on the list. They probably wouldn't make the list at all. They get old like the rest of you. They start to sag at some point, but the heart and spirit of a woman can keep her young in the eyes of her man forever.

"My Martha made me smile until the day she died, and I always found her desirable. After 3 kids and age, she was a little overweight.

She had wrinkles, stretch marks, cellulite, and gray hairs, but she was still beautiful to me. Our marriage stood the test of time. She stood up for me when your grandpa Jack told her he didn't like me, and she should find someone else. She raised my girls to be intelligent, independent, hardworking, God-fearing women.

"I worked long hours to make sure all of you had your needs and wants of life. Unlike many of the men I worked with, when I got off, I couldn't wait to get back to the loving home that she created for all of us. Some nights I'd do a little overtime and get off late. No matter how tired she was, your mother would fix me a hot plate when I got there. Your momma would sit and talk to me while I ate and ask me how my day went, like she was really interested in the boring life of a factory worker. Then, after I finished eating, she would take me upstairs and tell me how much she appreciated and loved me. She'd also do some other things fathers don't discuss with their daughters. I didn't mind working those 12- and 14-hour shifts because I knew what was waiting for me when I got home . . . some good lovin' from a good woman. Those things make a woman a woman, not her cup size. So, if you want breast implants, you get'em; but know they're not going to make you any more of a woman than you already are. You're Martha and Bobby Williams's baby girl, and you're all woman. But most of all, you're a child of God, the King on high, and that within itself makes you beautiful. God doesn't make mistakes, only masterpieces.

"I'm a blessed man. I don't have one regret when it comes to my family. God gave me more than one man deserves. You and your sisters are some kind of wonderful. You and Tasha are pursuing your dreams. We just have to get Vanessa on track. Even though she's not doing too hot financially, she's a good mother, and she's raising my grandchildren pretty well all on her own. That no-good Darryl, I could kill him for making my Nessa do this alone."

All I could do was smile. I always knew I had the greatest Daddy in the world, and once again, he'd reminded me why. We got up and made our way to the register to pay for our food. I grabbed my daddy's arm and held it tightly. I reluctantly let go after we were in the parking lot standing by his car. I kissed my aging father on the cheek and whispered in his ear, "I love you and thank you. I am who I am because of my wonderful mother and father."

He gave me a hug, kissed me on the cheek, and then opened the door to his Cadillac. It was his gift to himself when he retired 4 years ago. As he slid in the driver's seat and put on his seat belt, he looked up at me and said, "I'm your number one fan, and I'll always support you, Pumpkin. Now, go make some hits so you can buy me a Bugatti! Do those come with butterfly doors? If not, you have to get them to put some on just for me."

I giggled and tried to imagine my elderly father in a car with butterfly doors. "I gotcha, Daddy. I'm gonna make you proud," I replied.

"Pumpkin, you already have," he said. "Oh, and tell that boyfriend of yours I'm still waiting for him to ask me for your hand in marriage. How dare he think he can get the milk without buying the cow? And I can't believe you're letting him."

I rolled my eyes. "Daddy! Don't start."

"Okay, I won't ruin our wonderful breakfast by fussing, but you know I'm right. Bye, Pumpkin."

"Bye, Daddy," I said and watched him drive away.

When I got home, I decided to give some serious thought to whether I wanted implants. In order to see how the other half lived, I put the DD falsies in my bra. Then, I looked around and noticed the house was a mess. Tyler and I worked so much we didn't clean up the way we should. I turned on Janet Jackson's greatest hits to keep me company as I went about my duties.

I started cleaning in the kitchen and sang "Control" as I washed the dishes. Then I mopped the floor to "Rhythm Nation." The mop doubled as my microphone. I sang into the handle as if I was onstage performing one of my songs. At one point, I put the mop down and did the dance routine from the video that my friends and I once worked hours to perfect for a student talent show. I was surprised that I actually still remember it. As I bounced around on our tile floor, I felt the rise and fall of the falsies against my own breasts. I barely felt anything move when I danced before.

Our town house is small, but it's a dust magnet, and having a cat doesn't help either. I kept on bouncing as I proceeded to clean, dust, and vacuum the living room and dining room. Afterward, I headed upstairs to the bedroom. I stopped bouncing momentarily while I changed the sheets on the bed. I put on the bottom sheet, unfolded the top sheet, and gave it a good hard snap. As it fell into place across the bed, Tyler appeared on the other side of the bed with a large bouquet of flowers in his hands.

I smiled and began to reach for them. He suddenly dropped the flowers on the bed, ran over to me, and exclaimed, "You look great! Why didn't you tell me you were having surgery today? I would have come with you. How long until I can touch them? Do they hurt? I wondered what you would look like with big ole titties, and now I know. I got me a regular Pamela Lee Anderson. I can't wait to show you off!"

"You idiot!" I screamed. I picked the flowers up from the bed and hit him repeatedly in the face with them as hard as I could. He put his hands up as a shield and quickly backed away out of my reach.

"What is wrong with you, woman?! Have you lost your mind?"

I glared at him with my death ray vision and yelled, "No, but you are stupid!" I then slid my hand under my shirt, took out one rubber titty, hurled it at him as hard as I could, and followed it with the other. Unfortunately, I have bad aim and missed him entirely. One landed inside the closet. The other hit the dresser and tumbled to the floor near his feet. Tabitha, the cat, thought it was some kind of toy. She pounced on it and swatted it in between her paws.

The look of shock on Tyler's face migrated into disappointment, and then shame. I really thought he had my best interests at heart. Maybe Tyler wasn't the man I thought he was. I used to think I looked okay, but now I felt like Quasimodo in the *Hunchback of Notre Dame*. Does anybody know where I can find sanctuary? My feelings need protection.

He looked at me and said, "I'm sorry, Pussycat. I thought . . ." His voice trailed off.

I looked at him and snarled. He'd better be quiet. There were no words to fix what he had done, and he seemed to know it. Tyler headed toward the door of our bedroom and before exiting he said, "For what it's worth, you are beautiful. I love you, and my life would be empty without you."

I didn't bother to respond. Instead, I turned around and finished making our bed. It now had colorful flower petals all over it that I had to remove. Tyler had managed to make two messes in a matter of seconds. I heard his soft footsteps descend the stairs. I also heard the door open, and then close. I was glad that idiot left!

I stood there and stared at the rubber titty that was now the property of Tabitha. She was still swatting it between her paws and pouncing on it. I wondered if they were in me would she try the same thing. That would be painful. Had Tyler always been so stupid and insensitive and I was too in love to notice?

He didn't come home that night, which was fine with me because I didn't want to see him. I assumed he stayed at the studio. That's usually where he goes when we fight.

The next morning, I was awakened at 8 a.m. by the annoying sound of my cell phone ringing. I had no intention of answering it. That's what voice mail is for. I glanced at the screen to make sure it wasn't anyone important. When I realized that it was Melvin I answered.

"Babe, the record label sent over a couple of your pictures. You look fabulous. Bigger breasts really do look good on you. Did you make an appointment to see that plastic surgeon? I mean, you really look hot!" he exclaimed.

"No, Melvin, I didn't," I answered dryly.

"Well, what are you waiting for? Your new hooters are waiting. Go see him today, get an estimate, and then call me back. I may be able to get the label to foot the bill. Bye."

Had the whole world gone cleavage crazy? I guess it wouldn't hurt to talk to the doctor. It might even be the answer to my problems. If I got bigger boobs, then everyone would shut up about how much I needed bigger boobs.

I got up, rummaged through my bag for the number, and called the You, Only Better Cosmetic Surgery Clinic to make an appointment. The friendly woman on the phone said they'd had a cancellation that morning, so she could fit me in if I could get there in the next hour. I told her I'd be right over and got dressed.

A strange feeling of dread washed through me. I knew it was only a consultation, but I felt like I was about to walk the plank with humongous, hungry sharks below waiting to devour me. I also felt anxious, like Dorothy must've felt when she set off to see the Wizard of Oz. Maybe the doctor could make my wishes come true. All I wanted was to feel beautiful again. I wanted my man to look at me like I was desirable from head to toe. I wanted perfect strangers to not comment on my breasts—or lack thereof.

Once I arrived, the cheery woman who'd answered the phone gave me some paperwork and told me to have a seat. Sitting next to me was a gorgeous blond-haired woman who actually resembled Pamela Lee Anderson, but she didn't have that sparkle Pamela has when you see her on TV. She looked really sad. I completed my paperwork and handed it to the receptionist who instructed me to have a seat and told me when the doctor was ready, someone would call my name. I sat down and the blonde looked me directly in the eyes. She then looked down at my breasts, and then back in my eyes again.

"Don't do it," she said bluntly.

"Excuse me?" I asked.

"I know why you're here. Don't do it. I did it, and I've regretted it every day since. I hate these things. Since I got them, no one looks me in my face anymore. At least not at first. They look at them, and then look at me. I thought I would enjoy being sexy and voluptuous, but it's almost like no one takes me seriously now. When I go on dates, men are always looking at them and not listening to a thing I have to say. It's obvious all they want is sex, and because of the clothes I wear to try to show off my new, expensive assets, they think I'm easy. I thought I needed something to give me a little edge over the competition. You see, I'm getting on up in age, and I would like to get a husband before my eggs dry up.

"Take it from me, doll, you're beautiful already, without the tits. Don't get me wrong; implants have benefits, but unless you want attention drawn to that area all the time, don't do it. I used to think having small breasts was a curse. Now, when I look around, I see there are lots of gorgeous women with small breasts like that actress Kate Hudson, Chili of TLC, Zoe Saldana, and mega model Kate Moss. You remember how pretty Aaliyah was. It's a shame she had to die in that accident.

"*You* look like a model. 'Go to hell!' That's what you say to anyone that tells you that you don't look good exactly how you are. Only a demon from the pit of hell would seek to strip you of a positive self-image and lower your self-esteem. Yep, you tell that person to go back where they came from. You look them dead in the eye and say, 'Go to hell.' People are so vain and backward. We spend thousands of dollars trying to conform to the standards of a fickle society that doesn't care about us. No one can love you more than you. So, if you're happy with yourself, who cares what the world says."

I was about to respond, but a nurse called my name, indicating that the doctor was ready to see me. I looked at the blonde and said, "I appreciate your concern, and I'll take your words under advisement. You're beautiful, too, you know."

She smiled. I patted her on the hand before I grabbed my purse and followed the nurse into a small examination room. She told me to take off my clothes and put on one of those backless gowns and turn it around so that the gaping hole was facing the front. She then left the room so I could undress. The room was cold and my nipples became hard in a matter of seconds. I put on the gown, pulled it tightly together to close the hole, and sat at the end of the examination table with my feet dangling above the floor. After about 10 minutes, a handsome African American surgeon named Dr. Muhammad entered the room. I pulled my gown together tighter with my hands and kept them there. I hate showing my body to strangers, even if they do have MD at the end of their names. He introduced himself and sat in a chair opposite where I was sitting.

He looked to be about 50 years old. His hair was black and cut low with a few gray hairs sprinkled throughout. There was also some gray in his mustache. He was very handsome. I was almost sure I'd seen him somewhere before. He introduced himself.

"Let's see what we have here. Do you mind moving your hands?" he asked politely.

I moved them reluctantly. He opened the front of my gown, looked at me clinically through a pair of Versace frames, and then asked me a question. "Why do you want breast implants?"

"I'm an up-and-coming singer, and I believe bigger breasts would help my image, which would ultimately help my career," I stammered. I couldn't tell if I was stammering because I was nervous or because it was cold in there; but that's not a question you answer every day, so he shouldn't have been surprised the answer didn't come easily.

He continued to examine my chest. His hands moved across my breasts feeling the tissue. I hated being touched by strangers more than I hated being looked at. As soon as he stopped, I pulled my gown back together. He stood there and looked at me. It seemed like an eternity before he said something else.

"My profession is cosmetic surgery, but what I really specialize in is self-esteem, a positive self-image, and confidence. Many of the people, but not everyone, who come to see me think that all those things can be obtained through large breasts, high cheekbones, slimmer noses, thighs with no cellulite, tighter behinds, and flat stomachs. To them, a better body means a better me. They don't even realize that the problem isn't on the outside. It's really on the inside.

"You do have small breasts, but you are a small woman. Your breasts fit your body. You're what we men refer to as a slim goodie, Ms. Williams. If I wasn't married, I would ask you out," he chuckled. "I'm all for enhancing one's appearance for the right reasons, but you don't seem to have them."

"What makes you say that?" I asked.

"Judging from that apprehensive look on your face, you're not doing this for you. Women who really want cosmetic surgery can't wait to see me. They are giddy with anticipation. They barely let me get in the room before they fling open their gowns so I can get the examination over with and get them on the operating table. You, on the other hand, don't look happy to see me, and you're holding your gown together like I'm a rapist." He chuckled.

I loosened my grip on the gown. I guess I did look unhappy to be there. "I'm not sure this is right for me," I admitted.

"Then, you shouldn't change a thing until you are. I know who you are, Dawn, and I've heard your music. I enjoy live music, and I frequent a lot of the little clubs around town. I've seen you perform several times. The first time I saw you, I was captivated by your beauty. Then, you opened your mouth to sing, and I could have sworn I saw Jesus sitting over in the corner enjoying one of his angels sing. You have an amazing voice, and no breast enlargement is going to add or detract from that. In some people's opinion, bigger breasts may improve your appearance, but I don't care how big you make your breasts; if you can't sing, no one is going to listen to you very long anyway. Now, put your clothes on and go home. Take it from a man who has seen hundreds of women without their clothes on. There's nothing wrong with you, and I can't help you. I can't improve on perfection.

"Be glad someone sent you to me. I have plenty of colleagues who would've talked you into that surgery and five more you don't need to increase their fees."

At this point, Dr. Muhammad was smiling and so was I. A man who could've made thousands off me had declined to provide me service. He walked toward me. Once he was directly in front of me, he stopped, stooped down, and planted a kiss squarely on my lips. I didn't move. His behavior was unprofessional, but to my own surprise, I wasn't upset in the least. It was actually kind of nice. I'm sure Tyler wouldn't have thought so. Screw him!

Dr. Muhammad licked his thick dark lips as if he'd tasted something deliciously sweet and was trying to savor the last little bit of flavor from it.

"I hope I didn't offend you. Your lips are every bit as soft as I dreamed they would be. Please excuse my liberties. Thank you, Ms. Williams. You have allowed a married man with three kids and a spoiled wife to fulfill a small fantasy. I have a prescription for you. Every day, I want you to stand naked in front of a full-length mirror and tell yourself, 'I am beautiful.' As you look at yourself, focus on the parts of your body you like instead of what you don't like. Repeat the statement at least five times. Do you understand?"

I nodded my head up and down.

"Good. It has been a pleasure meeting you. You are free to go, and I look forward to watching your career progress."

Dr. Muhammad exited the room. *This fine, intelligent, successful man is a fan and not only that, he has fantasized about kissing lil' ole skinny, flat-chested me.*

There was a full-length mirror on the back of the door in the examination room. I walked slowly toward it and looked at my reflection. The weave Dontae did for me looked gorgeous flowing around my delicate shoulders. I let my gown fall from my body onto the hard white linoleum floor. I stood in front of the mirror and continued to look at myself. I cupped my small 34A breasts with my hands. *Who created bra sizes, anyway? Breast size is one of the few categories I know of where having an A is regarded as a bad thing.*

I scrutinized myself closely. My breasts really didn't look so bad. I'd had them since I was 16 and until yesterday, I didn't have a real problem with them. They didn't seem to have a problem with me. I let my eyes travel to the light stretch marks on my perfectly round buttocks. They are remnants from my high school basketball days. I then looked at my flat, tight abs. I've always loved them. I pulled my weave up and pinned it to the top of my head with my hands and admired my long neck.

"I am beautiful," I said. I tossed my hair over my shoulder the way women did in the L'Oréal hair coloring commercials I used to watch as a child. The one with actress Cybill Shepherd used to be my favorite. "Don't hate me because I'm beautiful," I said and smiled. I followed it up with the words, "I am beautiful." I said them again louder and more boldly than the first time. I took a deep breath and prepared to say them again, but I was interrupted by a loud male laugh coming from the other side of the door.

"Ms. Williams, you are supposed to do that at home. I told you to leave. I have women who actually want cosmetic surgery waiting to see me. I need that room," Dr. Muhammad said and laughed again.

My face flushed with embarrassment. I quickly dressed and walked into the waiting area. The blonde I was talking to earlier was still there.

"Go to hell," I said with a wink and gave her a thumbs-up.

She smiled at me and laughed. She really was very pretty. I wondered who'd told her she needed bigger breasts to get a man.

"Next time, say it like you got some balls, girl! That was weak!" she joked.

"I'll work on it!" I smiled back at her and exited the building. I decided to use those three magic words on Tyler and Melvin. If I had to, I would fire them both!

When I arrived home, all the blinds were closed to create the illusion of night, and the dining room table was set for two. Several candles were lit, two glasses of Mimosa stood ready to be consumed, and a delicious smell was wafting through the house from the kitchen. *Was he cooking a romantic breakfast? Who eats breakfast by candlelight?* Tyler appeared in the kitchen doorway in a blue Sean Jean shirt and grey slacks looking extremely sexy.

"Hello, Pussycat," he said and kissed me slowly on the lips. It's funny how something as simple as a kiss could make every thought I was having vanish from my head.

What was I going to tell him, again?

He handed me what appeared to be a greeting card.

"I made this for you." He walked back into the kitchen and left me alone to read it. I opened the envelope and extracted a computer-generated card with a picture of Tyler and me on our first date on the cover. I remembered that night vividly. He took me downtown to a restaurant called Swank. We had a wonderful time laughing, eating, and listening to live jazz. I knew that night he was going to be my man. There was a poem written in the card.

That night you looked beautiful in your flowing black dress
When I looked at you, I felt short of breath
I couldn't believe a woman so fine wanted some of my time
Hearing your sultry voice as you shared with me your dreams was sublime
Your infectious laugh possessed just the right timbre to fill up a room
Every time you spoke, I started to swoon
And later that night holding your hand in mine as we walked along the river, I listened to you sing softly
I knew right then there was no other woman for me
My bass strums along to the rhythm of your love
You're my gift from heaven above
My heart beats in sync with the beat of your heart
I pray the two of us will never part
I'm a slave to your plantation
A citizen of your perfect nation
A bidder of your will
Without you, I'd be ill
Your wish is my command
I love being your man
Fulfilling your desires is my duty
I live to squeeze and pleasure that booty
I love your lips, your thighs, those eyes, those hips that switch
Yeah girl, I'm whipped
Each day I'm blessed to breathe the fragrance that is you
Without you I don't know what I'd do
I'd be a puzzle with a missing piece
A carnivore with no meat

A human with no air
Without you, life would not be fair
I love you, Pussycat
What I said was whack
Please forgive me
I take it back
You're my superstar
And you're beautiful just the way you are

It was a little corny, but I loved it. Tyler slowly walked up behind me and gently slid his arms around my waist.

"I was a total jerk. I want to forget about the past 2 days and start over. Can we do that, Pussycat? Your body is absolutely perfect." He breathed seductively on my neck, and I felt a hand inch upward and begin massaging my left breast. "I love every single inch of you."

An ill-timed phone call came through and interrupted Tyler's apology. It was Melvin. I told Tyler to hold that thought. I needed to tell Melvin a thing or two, and it couldn't wait. As soon as I said hello, he started talking.

"Hey, babe. How are you? Did you go see the plastic surgeon? I e-mailed you the pictures. Did you see them? Don't you look hot? You should show them to Tyler. I talked to the label, and they said they don't think a little surgical enhancement would be a bad idea. They are even willing to pay for it. Of course, you know that's fancy terminology for we'll take it out of your royalties, but who cares? What do you think?"

My face tightened with every word that came out of his mouth. I couldn't take it anymore. "Go to hell, Melvin!" I screamed.

"What? What's wrong with you? I try to help you and you tell me to g—"

I cut him off and said, "Go to hell," again. "I am beautiful just the way God made me, and if you don't think so, then maybe I need another manager."

"Whoa! Hold on a minute. I didn't mean to offend you, Dawn. I thought this was what you wanted. Of course, you're beautiful. You always have been. I don't care how big your breasts are. I represent you because you're talented and you're going places. Maybe I jumped the gun. You don't need another manager; we've got major moves to make, me and you. I apologize. You know how excited I can get sometimes. If you don't want enhancements, then by all means, don't get them. I care about you. I saw how upset you were at the shoot, and I thought I was helping. The next time someone tells you to change anything, you come tell me, and I will put them in their place. I'm more than your manager; I'm your friend, and if I say something I shouldn't, then tell me. The last thing I want to do is hurt you, babe."

I breathed a sigh of relief. I didn't really want to lose Melvin. He's a pretty good manager.

"Thank you, Melvin. I would appreciate that."

"No problem, babe. Don't forget we have a studio session tomorrow at 6 p.m. Don't be late."

"I'll be there. Now, I have to go spend some quality time with my man. Bye, babe," I said mimicking him.

I ran back to Tyler and threw my hands around his neck. "Now, where were we?"

"I was right here," he said before kissing me deeply. Once again, every thought I was having disappeared.

One year later . . .

"And the winner for best new band group or duo goes to . . . The A Cup Club!!" yelled the announcer.

Can you believe it? I am at the American Music Awards with my band and family. After that whole breast implant ordeal, I went to my music label and told them I had an idea. I wanted to create an all-female band whose members had small breasts. My label loved it! They got behind me 100 percent and made it happen. Our whole purpose was to start a new movement that encourages women to love themselves as they are.

I'm the lead singer, and I have five of the baddest women who ever picked up an instrument backing me up. We named our debut album *Masterpieces,* and our first single, "You Know I'm Sexy," went to the top of the R&B and pop charts and stayed there for a full 10 weeks. People also loved our second single, "Love Thyself," and the third, which is an inspirational song called "In His Image." Our album went double platinum!

The best thing is that women all over the world are listening to our message. Fans of all shapes and sizes are showing us mad love wherever we go. Women who are underweight and overweight with big breasts, small breasts, potbellies, stomach rolls, big booties, no booties, stretch marks, cellulite, wide hips, missing in action hips, and wide noses are all coming to our shows and leaving feeling good about themselves. We have received and continue to receive tons of letters and e-mails from ladies who say they didn't like their bodies but our songs are helping to give them confidence and a more positive self-image. They are learning to love themselves more because of lil' ole me! God is using me to spread His message of love, and I'm so happy He is.

Now here we are in Los Angeles at the American Music Awards accepting our third award of the evening. This is one of the best things that has ever happened to me! One of the other things is Tyler and I got married about 7 months ago. God was pouring such amazing blessings into our lives we decided to do the right thing. We had a beautiful double wedding with my sister Tasha and her beau. We're doing really well. Tyler's band, Trifecta, is currently on tour with an award-winning R&B artist named Marshall Kennedy! Next month, The A Cup Club is going on a world tour to spread our message of self-love across the globe. My man and I are both making our dreams come true.

I rose to accept our latest award with pride. Tyler and my dad were sitting next to me and each stood to give me a hug as I passed them. They both looked handsome in their tailored suits. As I moved past my father, he leaned over and whispered in my ear, "Your mother would be so proud of you, Pumpkin. I wish she were here."

"Me too," I whispered back.

"When am I getting my Bugatti?"

"Soon, Daddy. Real soon," I laughed.

I was all smiles as I and the five other band members headed up to the podium to make our acceptance speech. I looked into the audience. This entire night seemed surreal. I took a deep breath and spoke loudly into the microphone. "I wouldn't be doing any of this without God. He is so good, and I feel beautiful. Thank you for making me just the way I am and saving my soul!"

Take Care of Those You Love

Be devoted to one another in love. Honor one another above yourselves.—Romans 12:10

It's Friday! There are several reasons why I love Fridays. For one, it's payday. Every other Friday I get a nice check to help pay my bills and fund my fetish for stylish clothes, shoes, and handbags. Friday evening is also the beginning of my weekend. I get to spend 2 whole days doing what I want to do, and it usually includes some quality time with my man, Aaron. TGIF! I really do thank God for Fridays.

This particular Friday began like any other. I walked into All Tech Media where I serve as a junior account executive. We are a company that specializes in helping small and large businesses harness the technology of new media to catapult their business into the stratosphere. I work in the division that handles new media marketing. I recently completed an assignment where I served as the lead on a very successful campaign for an ice-cream franchise company that is new to the market. In 6 months, we made the three new Nashville locations more profitable than any other market. Some of the other stores have been in existence for over a decade. The woman who bought into the franchise here decided to open three locations simultaneously. Rather than spending all her money on advertising solely with traditional media outlets such as television and radio, she wanted to implement an aggressive social media component.

I created a campaign that utilized Facebook, Twitter, Instagram, Pintrest, YouTube, and a small amount of publicity from local television, radio, newspaper, and magazines to let all of Nashville know about her business. I threw in a couple of bloggers to help tout the praises of the product. I also collaborated with an event planner to implement a couple of off-line contests for extra spice, and voilà! A successful campaign emerged. It went better than anyone expected. I knew selling cold ice cream during a hot summer with record-setting high temperatures wouldn't be the hardest thing to do, but I had to tell people why Eskimo Ice Cream was the only place to get it. That took some creativity. Our "Colder Than Ice" campaign offered free samples once a week to the first 200 people. Customers were lined up around the block to try their creamy treats. Most samplers liked what they had to offer and ordered a scoop or two before they left.

OK. Back to Friday. I arrived in our office suite and greeted one of the other junior associates. Fred gave his usual grunt. How he ended up in marketing, I will never know. That man has virtually no communication skills, and he's about as friendly as a bear that was interrupted while eating. I noticed that the other junior associate, Jordan, wasn't in his office. Most days he's the first to arrive and the last to leave. I also greeted our office assistant, Eric, who I share with Fred and Jordan. Until coming here, I had never worked with a man as administrative support, and I quickly realized how much more I enjoyed it. He wasn't prone to all the gossip and jealously I previously encountered with women. He wasn't interested in where I got my shoes or where my dress came from or who I was sleeping with. He wanted to know if he wrote my correspondence the way I wanted it written or if he should order croissants or bagels for an upcoming breakfast meeting. Eric was about helping me handle my business, and I loved it. The only time he offered his opinion on my personal life was when I asked. As a husband and father of two small children, he's able to give some pretty good advice concerning the behavior of men and relationships. Yep, having Eric as my assistant is a blessing.

I passed his desk as I headed to my office. He greeted me with a cheery, "Good morning, Felecia. You look lovely today." I thanked him for the compliment, and by the time I took off my suit jacket, put my briefcase down, and settled into my chair, he was in my office with a cup of hot coffee in my favorite *I'm A Good Woman* mug. He placed the beverage on a coaster and told me that the head of the company was in our area 10 minutes earlier looking for me. He said he wanted to see me as soon as I arrived. Good thing I'm on time today. He didn't say what he wanted, but he did say that it was important. That was odd. Mr. Tollison never speaks to me directly about business. He always does it through my supervisor, Mrs.

Taylor. I wondered what he could possibly want. I took three large gulps of my coffee and checked my makeup. Not too hot, just the way I like it. Eric is also good at remembering what makes me happy.

"Stop that," advised Eric. "You look good, Felecia. You don't want to keep the big boss waiting. I'll be at my desk if you need to talk after your visit."

"Thank you, Eric. I'll let you know how it goes," I said.

My office is on the third floor, and Mr. Tollison's is on the fifth. I swung by Mrs. Taylor's office to see if she knew anything about it, but she hadn't arrived. Neither she nor Jordan were in yet. That was an oddity as well. Was there a meeting that I didn't know about? I'm usually the last person to arrive.

I decided to take the stairs so I could get in some exercise and have a few more minutes to calm my nerves. I walked slowly, but my mind raced through the hundreds of reasons why I was being called to the big office. I knew I wasn't getting fired, and we don't usually get raises until our annual evaluation, so what could Mr. Tollison want with me? Two flights of stairs didn't provide enough time to figure it out, and there was no one I could ask.

Once I arrived at the gray metal door with a large five on it in bright yellow paint, I took a deep breath and opened the door. Five seconds later, I was standing in front of Mr. Tollison's assistant, Wilhelmina, informing her that my presence was requested. Her bun was pulled so tight at the top of her head that it looked like it should hurt. I was almost certain that's why her eyebrows were arched almost to her hairline, and she had a permanent attitude. Wilhelmina has been at the company since its inception 30 years ago. She is known around here as "Security". She takes her job as the boss's personal gatekeeper seriously, and *no one* gets in to see Mr. Tollison without going through her first. Rumor has it that one time an angry employee barged into Mr. Tolliver's office without an appointment, and she tackled him to the ground and pinned his arms behind his back until the official office security team arrived. You don't want to mess with Wilhelmina!

Wilhelmina instructed me to have a seat while she announced my arrival to Mr. Tollison via phone. She hung up the receiver and said, "He will see you now, Ms. Washington."

I walked into his spacious office and looked around. I had never been here before. I looked out of the large window on my right and realized that this office held a magnificent view of the next building. I guess that's what you get when you only have five floors, and the surrounding buildings have at least ten.

Mr. Tollison greeted me with a warm hug and told me to have a seat. That was another first. I see him in passing at least once a week, and usually all he has to say is, "How ya doing, Felecia?" Each time I tell him fine and ask him how he's doing. He always says something polite that means "Good, but I don't care to hold a conversation with you," and goes about his day. I never really liked that I had to call him Mr. Tollison, and he always called me by my first name.

It is well-known in this company that Mr. Tollison has no time for underlings. He pays his managers to deal with us so that he doesn't have to. If there is something he doesn't like about one of us, he tells our manager, and it is his or her duty to handle it. I still had no idea what he wanted, and I hoped whatever it was would only require a quick chat. I now needed to go to the restroom.

Mr. Tollison is a short man with a lot of power. What he lacks in height, he more than makes up for in stature. I wouldn't say that he was handsome, but I wouldn't call him unattractive, either. If I had a few drinks in my system I might even call him cute. He looks to be in his mid-50s. His stringy brown hair is streaked with gray and is beginning to bald in the middle. In an attempt to hide it, he combs his hair from the back to the front. I guess it doesn't matter if you have a ridiculous hairstyle when you have money.

A savvy businessman and mastermind marketer, Mr. Tollison started this company from the ground up. I've heard him tell the story of how it began in the kitchen of his mother's house, and then grew into what we see now. Five floors of prime office space with 50 employees that help him rake in about $500,000 a year. He's married with three grown children. He and his wife live in the suburb of Brentwood, which is known for its well-to-do residents.

"I've been watching you, Ms. Washington," he said, *Ms. Washington?* "And I'm quite pleased with the work you've been doing. You did an excellent job on the Eskimo Ice Cream account. That idea you had to have an Eskimo costume contest was brilliant! Who would have thought that people would actually come out in snowsuits in the middle of July just to get free ice cream for a year?" He chuckled. "Hundreds of people showed up to watch, and because it was hot, they all bought ice cream. Genius!"

"Why, thank you, sir. I was quite surprised at the overwhelming response myself. The man who showed up with his wife and kids in Eskimo attire and an igloo in the back of a refrigerated truck deserved to win," I said smiling.

"I agree. I know you're wondering why you're here. Well, I won't keep you in suspense. I'm going to tell you something in confidence. It's not for you to contribute to the office water cooler gossip. I'm telling you so that you will know what is going on in your department.

"It was recently brought to my attention that your superior, Mrs. Taylor, and your fellow associate, Jordan Banks, were carrying on an affair. The fact that Mrs. Taylor is married makes the situation grave enough, but both of them ignored our strict policy which prohibits fraternization between managers and their subordinates. I was forced to release both of them from the company yesterday. Whereas Jordan's position can remain dormant until we find a suitable replacement, Mrs. Taylor's cannot. With all the publicity we received as a result of your hard work, I must fill it immediately. We already have two other companies inquiring about social media services. I have decided that I want you to run the new media division. Do you think you're up to it?"

"Yes, sir," I said eagerly. "I am quite knowledgeable of all of the inner workings of the department. I know I can do an excellent job." *Who do you think was doing Mrs. Taylor's work while she was off frolicking with Jordan?* I thought to myself. I was a good employee and played dumb like I really believed they were always off strategizing and consulting about Jordan's accounts. I knew they were sleeping together after they both returned to work one afternoon wearing the same fragrance, Chanel No. 5. Also, Jordan's clothes were wrinkled as if they had been thrown carelessly on the floor and left there when they were perfectly starched when he arrived that morning. I never mentioned a word to either one of them. I did take careful documentation of what I saw in case I ever needed some leverage against either of them. It always helps to have an ace in your back pocket when people want to act stupid.

"Good. That's what I like to hear. Here are the keys to Mrs. Taylor's office. I want you to clean it out."

"Sir, if I may ask, why me? Shouldn't her assistant, Suzanne, do that?"

"I need discretion in this matter, and that woman is an incredible gossip. I never liked her, but Mrs. Taylor said she couldn't live without her and wouldn't let me fire her. She's on vacation this week, and when she gets back, I'm letting her go, too. I found out the reason Mrs. Taylor wouldn't let me fire her was because she was blackmailing her with the knowledge she had about her affair. Blackmail will not be tolerated."

Mr. Tollison shook his head violently while he made that last statement. Some of the hair he had combed to the front fell backward into its rightful place. He took his hand and smoothed it back upward before he continued talking. I bit my lip to keep from laughing.

"I do like Mrs. Taylor, but she made a gross error in judgment. As a favor to her, I have promised not to embarrass her by spreading the reason for her dismissal. Pack her personal belongings up, and I will have a courier take them to her. If you find anything linking her to Jordan, dispose of it. I don't want to know about it. You understand."

I nodded yes. "What shall I tell people when they ask why she left?"

"Tell them the truth. She is pregnant, and she has developed some complications in her pregnancy that require her to be on complete bed rest. That isn't uncommon when a woman of her advanced age becomes pregnant. That should suffice. Once the baby is born, you can tell everyone she decided not to return to work to focus on the joys of motherhood full-time."

This was beyond juicy. "And what about Jordan?" I probed.

"Again, you can tell the truth. Jordan was also sleeping with one of our clients, Ms. Danielle Wright of Wright Shoes. Feel free to share that inappropriate relationship, and that one only. I won't tolerate a gigolo in my company. That is not how you advance here. I learned years ago that mixing business with pleasure is detrimental to your career and productivity. You can't get anything done if you're in the bedroom instead of the workroom. Take my advice on that, Ms. Washington. My wife was once my assistant. You know what I did when I realized that I was falling in love with her? I fired her and gave her a 6-month severance package while we found her another job. By the end of the 6 months, I was so deeply in love that I married her, and she didn't need a job.

"Second to starting this company, marrying her was the best decision I ever made. As I stated, Ms. Washington, I need complete discretion in this matter. Your promotion depends upon it. This promotion comes with a 30 percent pay increase, a company cell phone, and credit card. You already have a 401k and full health benefits, and at the end of the first year in this position, you will be evaluated for a bonus based on performance. I am usually very generous with my bonuses. I'll have Wilhelmina send your contract to your office later in the day for you to look over. I need Mrs. Taylor's office cleaned out by Monday."

"Yes, sir," I said and began to rise to leave his office.

"One more thing," said Mr. Tollison. I froze at midrise.

"Yes, sir?"

"Congratulations! You earned this position even though the circumstances under which you received it weren't the most ideal. I have every confidence that you will do well. Mrs. Taylor likes you, too. It was her idea to promote you, and she said she is even willing to mentor you remotely during the transition. She also thinks you are very bright and considers you a friend. I hope you consider her one as well. I'm sure she's going to need one as she figures out what she is going to do without a job and a husband. He found out about the affair a week ago and moved out of the house. She realizes that she is the only one to blame for her demise, but this is an unfortunate turn of events, to say the least. However, I did give her a generous severance package to soften the blow. Mrs. Taylor was very good at her job. She's an excellent critical thinker, and she possesses top-notch people management skills. I will make a formal announcement about your promotion on Monday. For now, you will be listed as interim-manager. Enjoy your weekend, Ms. Washington."

I saw a flash of sadness in Mr. Tollison's eyes, but as quickly as it came, it was gone. He smiled.

"Welcome to the top-tier team of All Tech Media." Mr. Tollison stood and shook my hand. He then walked me to the door and shut it behind me.

It was no secret that he and Mrs. Taylor dated years ago when they were much younger, single, and trying to move up the corporate ladder. I had a feeling that Mr. Tollison's feelings for her had to do with more than business. She was lucky that her boss cared about her well-being. A lesser man would have used her situation as an example of what could happen when you disregard company policy. He was perfectly within his contractual rights to let her go with no severance pay. Based on Mr. Tollison's statements, it was probably safe to conclude that this child may not be her husband's. Poor Mrs. Taylor. She was no spring chicken. Forty-eight was an advanced age to have a baby. Her other two children were in college. Jordan was fine, but he wasn't fine enough to lose your job and your husband over. Not to mention the fact that he was sexing her and another woman at the same time. Actually, there were two other women. I knew for a fact that Jordan had a girlfriend who lived in Memphis. She was in Nashville at least one weekend out of the month to see him.

Whew, what a Friday! Mr. Tollison had nothing to worry about when it came to me dating anyone in the company. I was happily in love with Aaron. He worked as an IT specialist at a company located downtown. I fished my cell phone out of my purse to call him and tell him about my promotion news, but decided this was too good to tell him over the phone. Instead I would surprise him at work with lunch and tell him then. I knew he was there because he called me while he was on the expressway headed in this morning. He calls every morning. Aaron does a good job of letting me know his schedule so I feel secure in our relationship.   After my chat with Mr. Tollison, I went to the restroom. Then I returned to my office, checked a few e-mails, and started packing up my own things that was as I was moving Mrs. Taylor out I could move myself in. Her office was considerably larger than mine and my plants would enjoy more space to grow. If I came in for a few hours Saturday, I could have it all done by Monday morning.

At 11:30 a.m., I called Aaron to make sure he was at work. He usually takes lunch at noon on the dot every day. He answered the phone and informed me that he was hard at work and so busy that he probably wouldn't go to lunch. Perfect! I could pick something up for him, stop by to give him my news in person, and then be on my way. I decided to purchase lunch at Subway. We both love their cold cut trio.

Amazingly, the line at Subway wasn't very long. The smell of their fresh baked bread and cookies makes my mouth water whenever I'm there. I skipped breakfast this morning and couldn't wait to put my mouth on their tasty goodness. I ordered my sandwich on wheat bread with only mayonnaise, lettuce, and tomato. I ordered Aaron's with all the fixings on white bread. It always looks like an icky mess to me with all those toppings and condiments, but that's the way my baby likes it.

I arrived at his office at 12:15 p.m. and told the security guard on the first floor where I was going. I'd never seen her before. She must be new.

"Mr. Adams is not here," she informed me. "He didn't come in today."

"Miss, you must be mistaken. I spoke with him earlier, and he told me he was at work."

"Miss, you are mistaken. I only work at this location on Fridays, and the entire time I have worked here, Mr. Adams has never worked on Friday. I have been here 3 years. I know what I'm talking about." This flashlight cop had a major attitude for no reason. I kept my composure. I was having a great day, and I wasn't about to allow this woman to ruin it. "Are you sure?" I asked.

"Positive. May I ask who you are?"

"I'm his girlfriend."

She lost her attitude at lightning speed. "I'm sorry, miss, but please don't tell him I told you. If you two have a fight or break up, he could blame me, and I could get in big trouble. We're not supposed to give out personal information about employees. I'm sure he has a good reason why he told you he was here, and he isn't."

I didn't see how I could let him know he's been busted without telling him where I got it from. I didn't want her to lose her job, but I've been dating Aaron for over a year and not once had he mentioned that he was off every Friday. I knew he worked 10-hour shifts, but I was under the impression he worked 50-hour workweeks. He gets paid extremely well, and I assumed the additional hours were one of the reasons.

I said, "Thank you for the information," and walked away. I wasn't going to lie to her. I was about to act a doggone fool as soon as I figured out where he was.

I called him and he said, "What's up, sweetheart? You miss me so much you have to talk to me two times before 1 p.m.?"

"Yep. I can't seem to get enough of you. Did you get some lunch, yet?"

"Not yet. I was about to walk out the door and grab something quick and bring it back to my desk."

"Don't bother. I already picked something up, and I'm headed your way. I got Subway."

There was a suspicious pregnant pause. "Oh, baby, that's sweet but my coworker, Doug, is getting us something. There's no need for you to come. Just give the sandwich away."

"I thought you said you were going. It doesn't matter. Tell yourself or Doug not to bother. I'm almost there."

"Sweetheart, it's not a good day to come by. I'm swamped with work."

"But I have some really good news to share. It will only take a minute. It's too good not to share in person."

"Can it wait until tonight? We're going out to dinner, right? Just tell me then."

"Aaron, what's wrong with you? You're acting like you don't want me to come to your office. Is something wrong?" He was going to tell me the truth whether he wanted to or not.

"Honestly, nothing. I asked you not to come, and you are still pressing the issue. I'm swamped, and I don't want to break my concentration. It's not a good day, Felecia."

So, he decided to try the old pick-a-fight routine to get me to leave the subject alone. Not this time, buddy.

"Aaron, I know you're not at work. I just left your office. I wanted to surprise you with lunch and my good news. I know you don't work at all on Fridays. So, I need you to be honest with me and tell me where you've been going every Friday."

Another pregnant pause.

"What are you talking about? That dumb security guard probably didn't see me come in."

"Who said the security guard told me? Please stop with this horrible attempt to cover up your lies. Tell me what you are doing and where you go on Fridays."

Aaron took a deep breath. "Honey, can we talk about this when you get home?"

There was a lump forming in my throat. I had to get out what I wanted to say before the tears formed because it was going to be hard for me to say anything once the waterworks began. I wished I wasn't so emotional.

"Is it another woman? Have you been cheating on me the entire time we've been together? I need to know. Is Friday your secret rendezvous day?" I choked out. "Just tell me. No more lies, Aaron."

"No, it's not like that at all. It's not another woman. Well, it is, but it's not what you think."

"Then, explain it to me, and explain it to me right now. Who is this woman who isn't your other woman? If you don't, I will hang up this phone and never speak to you again."

"Okay, baby. I've been wanting to tell you for quite some time. Write this address down." I listened as he gave me an unfamiliar address, and instead of writing it down, I punch it into my GPS.

"It should take you about 15 minutes to get here. Calm down and don't pass judgment until I've explained everything. I'll be outside waiting for you."

The entire drive I thought of all of the horrible things I was going to do to Aaron and that chick he'd been messing around with. I had mace in my purse and a baseball bat in the trunk of my car. I played on a women's softball team, and my Louisville Slugger would come in mighty handy at a time like this. I found Jazmine Sullivan's "I Bust the Windows Out Your Car" on my iPod and turned it up loud. I needed some motivational music to help me get pumped in case I needed to go ballistic on him. I got angrier with each verse.

How could he? For the past year, I thought I was dating a wonderful man. I was actually dating a liar and a cheat. I arrived at my destination in about 15 minutes as he said I would. It was a place called Glenview Senior Village.

Senior Village? It was a retirement home. As far as I knew, Aaron had no family in the area. I found a parking spot. Before I could get out of my car, Aaron was at my door. He opened the door for me, and in spite of the obvious anger in my face, he gave me a hug and a kiss on the lips. He looked nervous.

"Baby, I'm not going to prepare you for this. I'm just going to show you," he said.

He took me by the hand and escorted me into the building. He then led me down a long hallway lined with rooms. Most of the doors were open, and I could see elderly people of various shapes and sizes milling around. Some were watching TV while others were lying in bed or sitting in a chair by the bed. Several of them were eating, which was to be expected because it was lunchtime. We stopped in front of a door that read Allie Adams on the door.

Allie Adams? The name sounded familiar, and Adams is Aaron's last name. I wondered why he never told me about her before.

We walked into the room, and there was a light-skinned elderly woman in a powder blue housedress sitting on the edge of the bed. She didn't even turn her head to acknowledge our presence. I immediately saw the resemblance to Aaron. He has her nose and narrow brown eyes. I used to tease him that he must be part Asian with such small, slanted eyes. She had long silver hair that was parted in the middle with a braid that hung on each side of her head. Even braided, her hair came past her shoulders. They were secured on the ends with a rubber band. Stray hairs stuck out from everywhere. It appeared as if they had been that way for several days, and it was time to rebraid them.

"Madear," said Aaron.

She still didn't turn and look at us. "Madear," he said again a little louder. "It's me, Sonny Boy."

The woman finally looked at us. "Sonny Boy, where have you been? I haven't seen you in a month of Sundays."

"That's not true, Madear. I've been here all day," he said.

"Oh really? Who's this pretty chocolate girl you got with you?"

"This is my girlfriend, Felecia."

"Hello, Felecia. How do you do? You have to excuse my clothes. I don't get dressed up much these days. I don't have much company. Sonny Boy should have told me you were coming, and I would have done so. Would you like something to drink? I can go into my kitchen and whip you up a glass of sweet tea if you like. I hope the drive to Greenville was nice to you."

I knew Aaron was originally from Greenville, Mississippi, but he hadn't been home since Christmas. Besides, we're in Nashville.

"No, ma'am. I don't want any tea. How are you?"

"Oh, I'm fine. Sonny Boy, who is this young lady you brought here with you?"

"Madear, this is my girlfriend, Felecia," Aaron said again.

"Oh, hello, Felecia. It's nice to meet you. Would you like something to drink?"

I gave Aaron a puzzled look. I already told her no.

"She has Alzheimer's," he whispered in my ear.

My heart went out to his mother. She looked strong and able-bodied, but her memory had grown feeble. I patted her hand and said, "No, ma'am. I'm not thirsty, but thank you for offering."

"Okay. Excuse me." She turned her head and looked in the mirror to her left. "I need to get up and comb my hair. Where's my . . . What do you call that thing I use on my head?"

"Madear, it's called a comb, or maybe you mean a brush," said Aaron. "But you look beautiful. There is nothing wrong with your hair."

"Oh, shush, boy. I know when my hair doesn't look right. Your daddy will be home soon, and I got to get ready for him. You know, I always make sure I look good when he comes home. The last thing a man wants to see when he gets home from work is an ugly-looking woman. Now, where's my comb?" She rose from the bed, walked over to the dresser, and started rummaging through drawers.

"Momma, Daddy died years ago. Please sit down and rest yourself. Your hair looks fine." His voice was patient and kind.

"Boy, my husband will be here soon, and I got to get my head together. Help me find a comb before I pull out my switch and whip you."

She looked at me as if she hadn't seen me before.

"Oh, hello. How are you? Sonny Boy, who is your friend?"

"I'm Felecia," I said. "I'm the lady Sonny Boy brought to comb your hair." I reached into my purse and brought out a comb.

A wide smile spread over the old woman's face. It was obvious that she was quite beautiful in her younger years. "Oh well, what took you so long? I got to look good for my Jeffrey. We've been married 40 years you know. I love that man. Come right this way." She led me to a chair on the other side of the bed, then she sat down and situated herself until she was comfortable.

"There should be some hair grease around here somewhere. Would you grease my scalp for me, too?"

Aaron whispered to me, "You don't have to do this."

I gave him a smile and told him to sit down. I didn't mind at all. Besides, his mother was much too pretty to sit around with her hair uncombed. I looked on the dresser and found a small jar of hair grease and a brush. They were next to a beautiful bouquet of flowers that was similar to the ones Aaron sent me Monday. Mine were red roses with baby's breath, but hers were intermingled with orange and white daises. Our red vases with a big white bow tied around them were identical.

"Those are some beautiful flowers," I said.

"Yes, they are. My Jeffrey gave me those. He knows how much I love daisies." She smiled.

I smiled at Aaron because I knew he was the one who sent them to her. I stood over Mrs. Adams and positioned myself in a manner that would easily allow me get to any side of her head. I undid her thick plaits. She had a beautiful silky, silver crown of hair. I talked to her as I brushed her hair, parted each section, and spread a thin coating of grease on her scalp. She told me about her days growing up in Greenville and how she and her husband met one day while walking to school. Her mind had transported her to a place where she was happy with the love of her life. She also talked about her only child, Sonny Boy, as if he were still a child, and it was her responsibility to care for him each day. She seemed to have no idea that at this point in her life it was her child that was taking care of her. She shared with me about how every day after school she had a snack of buttermilk and corn bread waiting on him when he got off the school bus. He was a true country boy. She raved about what a good student he was and how he stayed out of trouble. After I finished greasing her scalp, I did two French braids and secured the ends with rubber bands.

Mrs. Adams looked in the mirror and said, "Thank you. This is just fine. My Jeffrey will like this. He always did love my hair."

"I can see why. It's so beautiful," I smiled.

"How much do I owe you?" asked Mrs. Adams.

"No charge, Mrs. Adams. Sonny Boy already paid me."

"He did? He's such a good boy. He makes me and his daddy proud. You know he's going to be somebody important one day. I should introduce you two. You seem like a nice girl."

"Thank you, ma'am." She probably won't even remember she gave me that compliment, but I appreciated it just the same.

Aaron bent down and kissed his mother on the cheek. "Madear, I already met her, and I'm actually kind of sweet on her." He reached over, grabbed my hand, and pulled me close to him.

"Sonny, you are? Well, I'm happy for you. She seems like a nice girl. You bring her back to see me again. I'm hungry. Is it lunchtime?"

"Yes, ma'am. I'll go get it for you."

"Okay. I love you, son. You make me and your daddy real proud." She stopped and looked at me as if she'd never seen me before. "Who is this pretty girl you brought to see me?"

Aaron didn't say a thing. Instead, he ushered me from the room and closed the door behind us.

He draped his arm around my shoulders and kissed my temple. "This is where I spend my Fridays. Please don't be angry with me."

I returned the kiss, but I placed mine squarely on his lips. "I'm not angry, but why didn't you tell me sooner? You didn't have to hide this from me," I said.

"I'm very protective of my mother. I had to make sure you were a good woman with a kind heart who knew how to treat an elderly woman with Alzheimer's. As you know, I used to be engaged and Leslie was mean to my mother. She was a selfish, spoiled, insensitive brat. My mother was living with me when she was first diagnosed. Leslie acted like she didn't understand that she had an illness and grew angry with my mother when she couldn't remember something or do something for herself. I put her in this home because of her.

"As Madear grew worse, I realized that this was the best place for her, but sometimes I feel guilty. I would rather she be at home but I know she needs full-time supervision. I come and spend the day with her every Friday to let her know that I haven't forgotten her. I also stop in several other times during the week. Leslie began to demand that I stop spending my entire day here. She said it didn't make sense when she wouldn't remember I was here. She didn't seem to under-stand that I needed this time with her. My mother won't live forever, and my visits give me an opportunity to make sure that she's being treated properly.

"When we were in premarital counseling and Leslie discovered how much I pay for my mother to stay here, she demanded that we find someplace cheaper. I looked around, but no place offered the same level of care that they do here at Greenwood. I want my mother to be happy and comfortable. Leslie didn't seem to care. She was so focused on how much money would be coming out of our household for her care. I make plenty of money. The money I pay for her to live here wouldn't have impeded our quality of life in any way. When I refused to move her, Leslie told me that she wasn't going to marry a man with a mother who was a burden. I gladly ended the engagement and haven't spoken to her since. I wanted to tell you about Madear when I realized how caring and loving you are, but I hid her from you for so long that I didn't know how."

I gave Aaron a hug.

"I always knew you were a wonderful man who believed in providing for his family and taking care of those he loved. Don't worry about me leaving you because of your mother or how much money you spend on her care. I just got a promotion *and* a 30 percent raise. I don't need your money, and if you decide to marry me, I'm sure that between our two salaries we will manage just fine."

"That was your news? You got a promotion?"

I nodded up and down with a huge smile on my face.

"Baby, that's great! We gotta go out to celebrate! Your treat. I always wanted a sugar momma," he picked me up and swung me around.

I laughed. I knew he was kidding. The entire time Aaron I have been together he hasn't let me pay for one date. But celebrating did sound nice.

"I have an idea," I said. "When's the last time you took your momma out for a night on the town?"

"I don't usually take her out at night. Only on Fridays during the day."

"Do you think she would like going out at night. What's her favorite restaurant?"

"Madear likes any place with good spaghetti."

"I make really good spaghetti. You and your mother should come to my house at 5 p.m., and we'll celebrate as a family."

"Are you sure?"

"Of course I'm sure! Now that I know about her, there's no reason to hide her away here. I'm sure she would love to leave occasionally. We'll eat early so we can have her back before nightfall."

"Thank you. You're the greatest, Felecia."

"No. You are, and thank you for giving me another reason to love you."

Aaron came to my house later that evening with his mother, and we had a wonderful dinner. We talked, laughed and smiled. Mrs. Adams asked me at least 10 times what my name was, and I happily answered every time. She really was a joy to have around. I watched Aaron as he cut up her meatballs and moved everything where she could easily reach it. If she ever looked scared or confused, like she forgot where she was, he stopped what he was doing to assure her that she was safe. I enjoyed having Aaron's mother there with us. Madear was important to the man I loved, and in time, she became extremely important to me. That day gave me another reason to love Fridays.

I began to visit Madear as often as I could and made it my responsibility to make sure her beautiful hair was washed and styled regularly. Sometimes I curled it for her and let it fall around her face and shoulders. Her bright eyes would flicker and a wide smile would engulf her face each time I gave her the mirror to see her hair.

Unfortunately, Madear died the following summer. She passed in her sleep with a smile on her face. I knew it was because her Sonny Boy made sure she was well taken care of. The news of her passing came 3 months after our wedding and 2 months before a positive pregnancy test. I found out I was pregnant on a Friday. It's still my favorite day of the week.

Sex Is More Than Just Sex

Do you not know that your bodies are temples of the Holy Spirit, who is in you, whom you have received from God? You are not your own.—1 Corinthians 6:19

Dear Editor,

Let me begin by saying I love your magazine. Each month I can't wait to get the latest edition of *Diva Sense*. It is my dream to one day be featured among your pages for some fabulous accomplishment.

A few months ago you ran an article about how women should stop suppressing their sexual desires in order to be healthier and more fulfilled. It said that orgasms can decrease depression, stress, and anxiety. It also said that getting the big "O" helps to reduce blood pressure, boost immunity, and strengthen your heart—in short, good sex regularly may prolong your life. I can get with that!

The article also urged women to explore their uninhibited sexuality, whether it be self-pleasure, one-night stands, lesbian encounters, and/or multiple partners. It even talked about how the black church teaches that sex is ordained by God for marriage, and when some Christian women step outside what we believe is God's perfect will, we often feel guilty and are unable to enjoy the sex, therefore, being unfulfilled.

Well, I have a few issues with your article that I feel compelled to share with you. In your article, you advocate practicing safe sex, which is wonderful, but we all know that millions of us don't. And as long as sex feels good, there will be couples who get caught in the moment and don't reach for a condom.

I've lived on both sides of the street you're telling your readers to travel down. I've been the good Christian girl who tried her best to keep her legs closed until marriage. Well, that didn't happen. I fell in love at 23, lost my virginity, and came into the full knowledge of what makes the unclothed expression of two becoming one so wonderful. It was cosmic, magical, passionate, unbridled lustful love. I did feel somewhat guilty because of my Christian upbringing, but I was like a junkie on crack who couldn't wait until my next fix. So, not getting any from the love of my life wasn't going to happen.

Unfortunately, after 2 years, we broke up, and my sex life diminished. Having friends with benefits really didn't interest me. I decided that abstaining from sex would be the best thing for me to do. Besides, during my relationship, I had more than enough sex to possibly last me a lifetime or so I thought.

Over the next few months, I realized how hard it is not to have sex once you've become accustomed to getting it on the regular. Yet, I was determined not to give my cookies away to a man I didn't love. I read my Bible, I prayed, and I asked the good Lord for strength. I guess it also helped that I didn't have a boyfriend prospect in sight.

One lonely Saturday night I read your article. It made perfect sense at the time. You're not named *Diva Sense* for no reason, right? I was horny and needed to scratch my itch baaad. I had deprived myself of physical bliss because of my religious and moral beliefs, and I didn't seem any better for it. I was sad, I was lonely, and I went to sleep every night yearning for the touch of a man. I decided to take your advice and let go.

I picked up the phone and called an incredibly handsome young man I met a week earlier named Lawrence. We spoke on the phone a few times, and he seemed nice. He even made me laugh. He said he wasn't seeing anyone so he seemed like a good candidate for company. I decided to invite him over to watch a movie. I didn't exactly know what was going to happen, but I decided to go with the flow and let whatever was going to happen, happen.

As we were watching the movie, he leaned over and kissed me. It was nice. Then the kissing got more intense and his lips moved to other places. As he was gently kissing on my neck, I decided that I would abandon my morals and stop being the good girl. The past 6 months of celibacy had been a period of great self-discovery, but also lonely. This man was handsome, intelligent, funny, and kind, and he looked at me with the yearning intensity I remembered seeing in my ex-boyfriend's face. It was like I was a necessity—like food, water, air, and cable television. I realized how much I missed being desired. There's something very empowering about knowing that you are wanted.

As I felt waves of emotion rush over me that I hadn't felt in months, I said to myself *Just let go. Allow yourself this moment in time. Gift yourself this fine specimen of manhood. Take him into yourself and make him yours, even if it is just for tonight. You only live once, right? You can always pray and ask for forgiveness tomorrow.*

I did just that. When it was over I knew I didn't want just one night. It was unexplainable how a man I barely knew, knew how to use my body to communicate with my soul. Baby boy had skills! As I lay in his arms, I asked him if I could see him again, and he said, "Sure, Princess." Then, he kissed me gently on the forehead, and I went to sleep wrapped in his strong embrace with a warm fuzzy feeling that ran from the top of my head all the way down to my toes. I fell asleep in perfect bliss.

The next morning, I woke up alone, but I didn't care. I knew I'd see him again. I felt so good about that night that I forgot to ask for forgiveness. I was high off the essence of Lawrence, and I wanted to experience it again soon.

I had to tell someone about my cosmic experience so I called my good friend Diane. Diane and I didn't talk often, but every time we did, we picked up right where we left off. I told her every juicy detail. I told her how exhilarated I felt. How he made me feel. How with each thrust, I felt like I had taken off 20 pounds because with each movement I was releasing all the pent-up sexual tension I had been harboring since my breakup.

I noticed that Diane was very quiet while I told my story, but I didn't think much of it. I figured she was as into my recanting of my sexual experience as I was. She did ask me a few questions though. Things like his name, where I met him, and what he looked like. I probably went overboard with my description of how fine he was, but I couldn't help it. Lawrence looked like one of the sexy models you see on the covers of romance novels!

All day I kept reminiscing about the night before. But I was surprised and disappointed when nightfall came, and I hadn't heard from my lover. I just knew that after a night like we had experienced, he would call. How could he not? Surely he felt the surge of passion I felt. I became concerned. Maybe he was in in an accident, in the hospital, or dead.

The next day, I called him and he told me he had a confession to make. Lawrence had lied when he told me he wasn't seeing anyone. He was seeing another woman that he met on the Internet a few months prior, and he was interested in becoming serious with her. He told me they had a lot in common and he shouldn't have come over my house last night knowing he already had a great woman in his life. He said he was sorry, but he was most sorry that he had to inform me that the other woman was my friend, DIANE. He didn't know what the odds were that he would have a one-night stand with a friend of the woman he was dating, but this was a problem he had to fix. He also apologized for putting me and Diane in that predicament, but in order for him to salvage things with her, it was best that we didn't communicate anymore. I gave him a few choice words that were deserving of a liar and hung up the phone in his face. I then called Diane.

She told me she put two and two together while we were talking and she started to say something on the phone, but decided to talk to him first to make sure she was right. When she called Lawrence, he initially tried to deny it, but she had too many details. When he realized he couldn't make his lie work, he confessed. He apologized profusely but pointed out that they weren't in a relationship, so technically, he still had the right to see other people. But he would make it up to her somehow. He then made Diane promise not to tell me because he wanted to "be a man about it" and explain the situation to me himself.

I felt used and disgusted. Did this man *really* give me one of the best nights of my life and then tell me it was a mistake? Did I really sleep with someone who was also sleeping with one of my friends? I explained to her that I would have never let him touch me if I knew they were dating. Diane said she understood, but it still bothered her that he would sleep with someone else while sleeping with her and she hated that it was me. And even though Lawrence was as wrong as skinny jeans on a man, she liked him a lot and had no intentions of ending things with him. She could actually see herself marrying him some day.

She said, "I'm sorry he lied to you, Leigh. I'm sorry you got hurt, but I'm holding onto him. I know this is going to make it hard for us to be friends now, but he's good to me. He makes good money, and he's sweet. You know how hard it is to find a man like that. What he did to you wasn't cool, but he's always treated me right. Then she said something the cut me almost as deep as Lawrence's deed. "By the way, he said the sex wasn't all that good anyway. I think the word he used for you was frigid. Stop flattering yourself thinking that you two had something special. It was just sex."

I hung up the phone confused and hurt. I wondered if he really said that or was she merely being mean? She had to be lying. The sex was great! She wasn't there. I know what I felt, and I saw his reaction. The way his eyes rolled up in his head and had trouble forming his words. He sounded like he had a speech impediment. I couldn't believe she abandoned our friendship for a man. Had she really told me that she didn't care that he hurt me and that as long as he didn't hurt her, it was okay? When did she become so cold? In my mind, Diane should have had my back. I'm her girl! I mean, if a female hit her in the club, I wouldn't care that she didn't swing on me. I would help her whoop that heifer's tail and ask who she was and why she hit her as we sat in jail waiting for someone to bail us out. When my friends hurt, I hurt.

Within 24 hours I lost my lover and my friend. I kept thinking about Lawrence for months. He and I had an amazing connection that night. When I woke up the next morning, I was on cloud 9. Now my high has descended into the valley of the shadows of emotional death. I eventually had to admit to myself that what was shared was a sin called lust, nothing more. Lawrence never cared for me. It's hard accepting that you were a collision on the hit-and-run highway. He planned on sleeping with me and continuing to see Diane the entire time.

I'm a big girl, and I can accept the consequences of my actions. I tell myself if I had held on a little tighter to my principles and religious beliefs, that wouldn't have happened. If I had taken the time to get to know him, I probably would have realized I wasn't the only woman in the picture. I have no one to blame but myself. Throwing caution to the wind to get the big "O" turned out to be a big mistake.

Thanks for the horrible advice, *Diva Sense*. But there's more to this story.

Three months later, I went to see my gynecologist for my annual pap smear. Two days later, she called me to inform me that I had HPV.

"What the hell is that?" I asked.

She told me that it is the most common STD on the planet and it comes from having contact with genital fluids. I had never even heard of the human papillomavirus until then, but even more perplexing, I'd never had sex without a condom! My ex-boyfriend was a stickler for that because he wasn't ready for kids, and I made sure Lawrence used one. I thought if you used a condom you had no worries! She explained to me that condoms aren't 100 percent effective against pregnancy and STDs. It's more like 98 percent. They lower your risk, not prevent it. The only way to completely guard against those things is abstinence. I was having the worst luck!

My doctor went on to explain that the HPV caused some abnormal cells she called dysplasia that could lead to cervical cancer if left untreated. She suggested that we try something called cryotherapy to get rid of them. During the outpatient procedure, she would use an instrument to temporarily freeze my cervix, and when it "unthawed," I was supposed to have this watery discharge for a few days, and the abnormal cells should remove themselves in the discharge.

The day of my procedure, as I lay on the table in a cold room shrouded in a thin hospital gown with my legs wide open and my gynecologist in between them inserting something in there that I didn't want to be there, I looked at the ceiling and wondered how I got into this predicament.

Sex, that's how! I prayed to God for help. I didn't want to be there. I didn't want to go through this, but I didn't have a choice.

The release of that discharge was the nastiest feeling I have ever encountered. My body secreted this watery yellowish discharge for days. I thought it would never end! I felt like I was constantly peeing on myself, and I had to wear huge maxi pads so I wouldn't soil my clothes. I changed my pad every few hours when I felt it getting full. I felt gross! I actually did a praise dance when the discharge finally stopped. It lasted a little over a week. I went back for another pap to make sure the abnormal cells were gone and a few days later received a call that the abnormal cells were *still* there.

Can you believe that I went through that torture for nothing? My doctor suggested that we try a different method called the LEEP. It uses a small electric current to scoop out the abnormal cells in cervical tissue. I couldn't help but continue to chastise myself. If I had kept my legs shut, this wouldn't have happened. As I write this letter, I'm waiting for the results of another pap smear to see if the LEEP worked.

I wrote all this to say, how dare you talk about sex like it's just sex! That's the problem with our society; we have diminished an act that was meant for the marriage bed to mere recreation between strangers as if it were a pickup game of basketball at the neighborhood playground or spades in the community center. Then, you attacked the black church—the foundation upon which many of us cling to, to get through the hard times. Aren't we hypocrites? We want God when our lives are falling apart, but when He and His rules for living interfere with our definition of having a good time, we want Him to disappear. Who do you think got me through this harrowing experience? Who do you think put His arms of protection around me and made sure I didn't contract something a lot worse than HPV?

I was a fool to listen to you. You had clinical experts cosigning all through the article. I figured that they have years of experience on the subject, so they must know what they're talking about. I told myself, *Stop being such a square, Leigh . . . Have some fun . . . Have a one-night stand . . . It won't hurt anything. You only live once. YOLO!* WRONG! WRONG! WRONG!

But it's not what you said that makes me so angry. It's what you didn't say. Although I don't dispute the benefits of a good orgasm, I think your story only presents one side of the equation. You only gave the benefits and not the consequences. Your article fails to acknowledge the physical, emotional, and psychological factors that can come into play when a woman is given an orgasm by the wrong man. How do you think I felt when a man I had sex with had no desire to see me again afterward? He discarded me like I was a piece of tissue he wiped his behind with. Diane severed all ties with me, too. She said she doesn't blame me because I was a victim of dishonesty, but it's hard for her to be around me because it's uncomfortable knowing that I slept with her man. They are now a couple, and I hear they're talking marriage. Guess who won't be invited to her friend's wedding?

Now, back to you. Your article failed to mention the alarming rate that HIV and AIDS cases are ravaging the black community. Some of these cases are African American women who were exploring their sexuality, and they've had so many partners that they can't begin to figure out who gave it to them or how long they've had it. I shudder to think how this would have turned out if I had gotten pregnant, but there are millions of women who weren't so lucky. I'm sure there are millions of illegitimate children who have been conceived from one-night stands between people who were just having a little fun. That night of fun turned into a lifetime, and we have yet another single mother to add to the statics. And possibly another woman hollering about her trifling baby daddy who doesn't pay child support or spend time with his child. The truth of the matter is, if she took the time to get to know him before she gave him some, she probably would have known that he was broke and trifling before she birthed someone with his DNA. Do I sound mad? I hope so, because I am!

I acknowledge that I made the decision to indulge in sex with a man I did not know, but I based my decision on information I received from what I thought was a credible resource. In the future, please be more responsible. It is unwise to tell women it's all right to engage in anything goes intercourse simply because it feels good. If a woman chooses to have a one-night stand, an orgy, or a lesbian experience, that's her decision, but she should know that there could be serious consequences to her actions that she should be prepared for and willing to accept if they should happen. Sex is more than just sex! Believe me, I now know that if nothing else. How could you reduce an act that can result in the creation of a life, the ending of a life through STDs, or emotional and mental damage to such a trivial thing?

Somewhere we as a society have gotten it twisted. Yes, sex is fun, but there's so much more to it than that. There's a reason God created sex as an expression between a virgin husband and a virgin wife. He wanted to spare us the pain and regret that has torn my emotions to shreds and jeopardized my health. I'm also sexually traumatized. I'm scared to let another man touch me. I gave up the goodies, and now I have no man, I'm battling a STD, and I lost one of my best friends. Do you have any suggestions in your magazine on how to fix that?

Sincerely,

One pissed-off reader named Leigh

P.S. I dare you to print this in your editorial section! Help keep someone from going through what I did because of your irresponsible journalism.

Mentorship is Mandatory

As iron sharpens iron, so one person sharpens another.
—Proverbs 27:17

Debra loved visiting her foster mother. Ceclia Antoinette Wade, better known as Momma Cee, was one of those warm spirits who never met a stranger. At least 70 years old, Momma Cee didn't look a day over 50 and most days behaved as if she were even younger. She could line dance with the best of them, and her mind was as sharp as a tack. She was often called upon to share her wisdom and her delicious home cooking. Momma Cee loved people, and people most certainly loved her.

For the past 5 years, she served as tutor at a local high school. She sees it as her job and thoroughly enjoys it. According to her, hanging with the young folks is her secret to looking and feeling young. Sometimes the words young folks used were a little foreign to her, so to relate better to them, Momma Cee started watching popular television shows and surfing celebrity news web sites. Once she learned what the words meant, she used them too. Some of the things that escaped her lips made Debra want to blush.

Debra walked into Momma Cee's two-story brick house in the center of a predominantly black neighborhood in St. Louis and found Momma Cee sitting in front of her computer surfing the Internet.

"Hey, Momma Cee. What are you looking at?" she asked while giving her a quick squeeze around her shoulders and a peck on the cheek.

"I was just reading about this girl they call Superhead."

"Really? Why do they call her that? Does she have a big head or something?" Debra asked, already knowing the answer.

"That's what I thought at first, but naw, baby. She got that name from giving oral sex to celebrities. She even wrote a book about it."

"You can't be serious!" Debra exclaimed in mock shock. She was always amused when Momma Cee talked about the pop culture she picked up.

"Fraid so, baby. This poor child was so mixed up that she thought in order to get what she wanted in life she had to drop to her knees, look the one-eyed snake dead in the face, and then kiss him. The reason I looked her up is the boys been calling this girl at school that, and every time they say it, she gets real shame-faced and quiet. When I asked one boy why they called her that, he started laughing and said she opens her mouth a lot. I decided to do some investigating, and this is what I come up with.

"It seems that women have no shame these days. Monica Lewinsky and now this child. Back in my day, we didn't do oral sex. You was looked at as real nasty if you did it, but even if you did it, it wasn't something you would tell people. What you did was between you and your man. This child here done put all her bedroom business in the street for a fee. Seems she made a best seller out of wetting celebrity whistles. Now that I know what superhead means, maybe I can talk to this girl and find out what's going on with her. I can tell something ain't quite right with her. I think she has problems at home."

That was Momma Cee for you. She was always trying to save the world one young person at a time. She saved a lot of people that way, even Debra. Debra's mother, Diane, was in foster care and 14 years old when she had her. Momma Cee took both of them in and raised them like her own flesh and blood. But by the time Diane was 18, she decided she didn't want to be a mother. She ran off and left Debra with Momma Cee. Said she was going to Hollywood to become a star but nobody ever saw her on television or in the movies. Actually, nobody ever saw or heard from Diane again.

Momma Cee raised Debra all by herself. She made sure she had everything she needed, especially a good education. Debra was a smart child. She graduated in the top 10 percent of her high school class and received a scholarship to the University of Arkansas in Pine Bluff. On the day she left for college, Momma Cee surprised her with a bank account full of money. She saved the money she got from the state to foster parent Debra to help send her to college. In there was more than enough to cover the expenses her scholarship and financial aid didn't cover, like dorm fees, food, and transportation.

While there, Debra took a communications class and discovered she was really good at reporting and the camera liked her. She made broadcast her major. By the time Debra graduated, she had completed an internship with a local news affiliate and another one at CNN in Atlanta. She took another internship in New York and worked her way up to news anchor within 5 years, and she won two Emmys for her reporting.

Things were going good for Debra. She was making six figures, and she was a household name among New Yorkers and those in some surrounding areas. Yet, when Momma Cee let her high blood pressure and diabetes get out of hand and ended up in the hospital for a week, Debra decided that it was time to move back home to St. Louis and asked the local news station to find a job for her so she could be close to home. They were so thrilled to have a reporter from a top 10 market interested in them that they gave their longtime black female news anchor the boot and replaced her with Debra.

The St. Louis audience loved her, and now, 2 years later, Momma Cee is doing much better and Debra has no interest in moving. Debra convinced her to improve her diet and incorporate exercise into her weekly activities. Momma Cee started taking line dancing and yoga at the local YMCA at least twice a week.

Debra also enjoyed being at home. She enjoyed the less hectic living of St. Louis as opposed to the fast city life of New York. Although she missed the full social life and abundance of activities to choose from, they couldn't hold a candle to being close to Momma Cee. The old lady was such a jewel. Plus, Debra's job agreed with her. She made a nice salary and lived in a luxurious condo located downtown and drove a new Mercedes that she leased and traded in every 2 years. Everything that touched Debra Stark's body was designer, from the Versace lingerie that covered her behind to the Manolo Blahnik slingbacks on her feet. She worked hard for her money, and she saw no problem with reaping the benefits. One of her favorite sayings was, "Don't mistake this attitude for conceit; it's confidence, baby, and it never looked as good as it does on me."

Momma Cee's voice jolted Debra back to the present. "Baby, the Get Right program my church member works with is looking for mentors again, and I think you would be perfect. I could si—"

Debra abruptly cut her off. "Momma Cee, you know I don't have time. Especially for no bad as all get-out ex-gang members. We just did a story on how they broke in this old lady's house, stole all her jewelry, and raped her."

"That's *exactly* why they need mentors, Debra. So someone can show them a better way to live and get paper. That way, they don't have a reason to return to that thug life."

Debra laughed. "*Get paper?* Momma Cee, you'll repeat anything those kids teach you. I wish you would quit. The children at that school get worse every year, and you keep going. I'm worried about you. Let me set you up as a tutor at a nice private Christian school."

"Excuse me, Ms. High and Mighty, but didn't you graduate from that *same* school in the hood?" Momma Cee looked sternly at Debra while she spoke.

Debra sighed. "Yes, but it was different then."

"No, it's not. It's still a place where children go to learn, and that's why I'm there to help them learn. Those children need me. They are a product of their environment. Everyone wants to blame the kids for the way they turn out, when you should be blaming the parents. My job is to show them a little love and guidance and to let them know they can make something of themselves despite their circumstances. And where do you get off acting like you are better than them? It could have easily been you. Did you forget that you were a child of a teenage mother who abandoned you?"

Debra closed her eyes. She hated when Momma Cee brought up Diane. As far as she was concerned, the woman was dead. She was only 4 when her mother abandoned her. Debra could barely remember what she looked like. As a child, Debra used to dream that some beautiful woman in a white limo would come by her school and announce to everyone that she was there to pick up her daughter, Debra. Diane and Debra would then have a tearful reunion, and Diane would whisk her away to Hollywood and introduce her to all of her rich celebrity friends.

That never happened. As far as Debra was concerned, the only place where Diane could be considered her mother was on her birth certificate. Her real mother was the elderly woman sitting in front of that computer screen.

Momma Cee noticed the faraway look on Debra's face. "Baby, I hate to bring up a painful past, but I swear, the more money you make, the harder you try to act like you've always had it. I didn't raise you to be uppity," she said while shooting Debra a disapproving glare.

Debra shook her head. "They didn't need metal detectors or police officers in the school when I went there. Besides, I think I do enough. I give to about 15 different charities a year. I'm always going to charity dinners and balls and events, and I donate my time as an MC regularly. Just last week, I MC'd a Masquerade Ball benefiting the March of Dimes," Debra explained.

Momma Cee turned back to her computer and clicked her mouse before turning her attention back to Debra.

"You give from a distance, baby. You aren't giving of yourself by spending time with the people who need you most. Those rich folks in their costumes don't need you. You are becoming detached from your roots. When's the last time you even spent time with someone that was less fortunate than you? You spend all your time with rich people who probably could care less whether you live or die. The only reason they associate with a little colored girl like you is because you're on the news. If you were just Debra the former foster child from the hood, they would have nothing to do with you, and you know it!"

Momma Cee saw the look on Debra's face and realized she hurt her feelings. She softened her tone as she continued. "Baby, I'm proud of what you've accomplished and thankful for everything you do for me. You go out of your way to make sure that I eat right, exercise, and take my medicine. You are always buying me nice things that I would never even think to buy for myself, but it seems somewhere along the way, you forgot the value of reaching back and helping others. To whom much is given, much is required. For a woman in your position, mentorship is mandatory. Take the lessons you've learned and pass them on to the next generation. I don't ask you for much. Could you *please* do this *one* thing for me? I hear this young lady they want you to work with is a real sweet girl, and you only have to see her a couple of hours per week and call her from time to time to check on her. It'll do your soul some good. Please, baby?" Mama Cee stood up and gave Debra a kiss on the forehead like she used to do when she was little. Debra smiled. Momma Cee smelled like Jergens lotion and rosewater.

"I never could say no to you. Okay, I'll do it, but I want somebody with some sense and some morals. I don't have time for ignorant, fast-tail little hoochies or hoodrats. I want somebody with some potential that looks like she's going places. Now, I gotta get back to work."

"I'll bet she's a fine girl who just got caught up in a bad situation. Her homies probably talked her into doing something illegal, and she got caught. My church member knows who you are and what you represent. I'm sure she's pairing you up with someone wonderful."

"I bet," Debra mumbled as she walked out the door wondering what in the world she had signed up for.

Debra agreed to meet her mentee 1 week later. She asked the young lady to meet her at an exclusive downtown restaurant as a way to share with her a fine dining experience. She almost spit out her Perrier water when she looked up and saw Nyeaylashay (Nī-ā-lăh-shāy) Caprice Classic Ruffin for the first time. She could only be described as ghetto fabulous. Debra never suspected for one moment that she might be an embarrassment. It was obvious Nyeaylashay was trying to impress her, and if they were in the middle of a hip-hop video, she may have succeeded. But they were not. They were in one of the most exclusive restaurants in downtown St. Louis and surrounded by upper-class individuals who were all sitting with their mouths gaping open as they watched this spectacle of a human being move toward Debra's favorite corner table.

Debra had to think fast. Her first impulse was to grab the young lady and hightail it out of there before she saw someone she knew. Her second thought was to have her sit down and eat lunch under the shield of the crisp white tablecloth. It was long enough to cover her short black spandex skirt, gold belt with the enlarged *100% BITCH* buckle, and 5-inch black stilettos accented by gold chains dangling on each side. But it would not cover her too small hot pink top that obviously hid a push-up bra that was pushing her medium-sized cleavage up and forward. It also wouldn't hide the tattoo of Jesus being crucified on the cross that covered the expanse of her left arm and the one on her shoulder that read *Artemis*. Nyeaylashay's whole person screamed *I'm more qualified to drop it like it's hot* in the strip club, rather than work in television news. Her right arm was less dramatic with the word *honor* placed inside of a circle but the table wasn't going to hide it either or the layers of makeup that was smeared on her face. The array of pink, purple, and black colors over her eyebrows wasn't so bad, but the lips lined in black, and then covered in clear lip gloss made her appear as if she had kissed a grease can earlier that day. Her hair was standing all over her head in what used to be a faux Mohawk style with 42 pieces of weave that should have been retired at least 2 weeks ago. It was ghastly, and Debra was mortified.

I could just ignore her thought Debra, but then she remembered that she was Debra Sparks from Fox 2 News. She was welcomed into the homes of thousands of viewers every day, and even if she did not know any of the people in the restaurant, it was guaranteed that at least half of them knew her. At least they believed they did since they saw her every evening.

Debra decided her best bet was to leave because she could tell as she approached her table Nyeaylashay was already feeling uncomfortable with the attention she was getting. She had to do this tactfully so as not to hurt the young lady's feelings while still protecting her reputation in the process. She grabbed her Coach bag from the chair on her left where she carefully placed it when she arrived, removed a $10 bill to cover her water and the tip, and exited the table.

She walked up to Nyeaylashay and said, "Hello, I'm Debra Sparks. I assume you are Nyeaylashay," while extending her hand.

"Yeah, but most people call me Nay Nay. It's a pleasure to meet you. I watch you all the time. I wanna be just like you," Nyeaylashay said slowly while looking around at the people looking at her.

"Thank you," said Debra. She gently touched Nyeaylashay's arm, turned her around, and began guiding her toward the door. "Well, today's your lucky day, Shay. Do you mind if I call you Shay instead?" She gave her a nickname that seemed less hood right on the spot and did not wait for her to say if she minded.   "I just got called to do a story, and I'm taking you with me. You say you want to be a journalist? Well, there's nothing like on-the-job-training. Are you up for it?"

The newly named girl gave her a grin that covered her entire face and began nodding her head up and down.

Great, at least no gold teeth, Debra thought to herself.

"Well, let's go!"

As they approached the valet stand, Debra took out her cell phone and texted the words call me to Peggy, one of the station producers and a close friend. She then handed her keys to Martin. He was the 17-year-old nephew of the restaurant's proprietor, and he worked there on the weekends parking cars. He could barely grasp her keys without dropping them as he stared at Nyeaylashay's protruding cleavage and wide bottom being hugged tightly by her skirt. It was clear Nyeaylashay thought he was handsome by the way she batted her eyelashes and smiled sweetly at the young man. Debra had to admit she was an attractive young lady with a nice figure, but in that getup, she screamed *I'll do you in the backseat for $5.*

Yet, something told her that she was not a slut. Debra did her homework and read Nyeaylashay's file. She was smart. She graduated with honors from high school one year earlier but she had also been in a gang since she hit puberty. Her record was littered with petty crimes, such as theft and minor assaults. Most of them she incurred while she was with the other gang members. So, she was a smart thug. For the past 7 months, she had been in the Get Right program. Get Right was designed to get youth such as her out of the gang life, and after successfully completing the first phase, they could be assigned a mentor in a field they wished to pursue. Shay requested someone in the news because she wanted to be a journalist.

Martin soon returned with Debra's convertible Mercedes. Just as they buckled themselves in and were pulling away from the restaurant's covered entrance, Debra's cell phone rang. It was Peggy calling as instructed.

"What's up, girl? How did it go?"

"I'm on my way, boss."

"On your way where?" Of course, Peggy had no idea what she was talking about, and Debra didn't give her instructions to play along in her text.

"Oh, you don't need me anymore?" Debra continued. "I'm not that far. I can be there in 15 minutes."

"Debra, we are off today. What in the world are you talking about?" Peggy said, more confused than ever.

"I understand, but if you need me, I'm here. See you tomorrow. Bye."

Peggy then realized that she was being used to get Debra excused from a situation. She did the same thing to her last week while on a disastrous blind date. She hung up the phone knowing that her friend would call her later and explain how her mere phone call saved the day.

Debra looked over and saw the disappointed look on Nyeaylashay's face. She hated to do that to her, but there was no way she could have continued to sit in that restaurant with her looking like that. She was also afraid someone might have made a rude remark before Debra had a chance to properly address her fashion faux pas.

"I'm sorry, but that was my producer, and she just took me off that assignment."

"I understand," her mentee said softly.

"I'll make it up to you. Are you still hungry?" asked Debra.

"Yes, ma'am." She seemed to perk up a little at the mention of food.

"How about we get something to go, and then go to one of my favorite parks?"

"The park? I'm not much of a nature girl," said Nyeaylashay.

"Nature?" laughed Debra. "Girl, I'm taking you to a city park, not camping in the woods. I keep a picnic blanket in my trunk for nice days like this. I love eating and people watching in the park."

Since lots of women exercised in the park half-naked Debra figured Nyeaylashay's outfit wouldn't be too much of a spectacle there. They drove to her favorite deli, picked up some sandwiches, chips, and sodas, and drove to the park. This one contained a lake, a walking trail, and a playground. After finding a parking space, Debra popped her trunk, pulled out a large picnic blanket, and headed to a shaded spot under some trees near the lake. She spread the blanket out, took off her shoes, and instructed Nyeaylashay to do the same. Once they were seated, the two of them began quietly eating while watching ducks play in the murky water.

"I like it here. It's quiet, real peaceful, not at all what I'm used to," said Nyeaylashay.

"Really? What are you used to?" asked Debra.

"At my aunt's house where I used to stay, there was always people in our home, so it was generally pretty noisy. We always had at least 3 of my little cousins living with us at a time. Sometimes their parents would come back too. I had my own room, but even with the door closed, I could hear the noise."

"What about the house where you live now?"

"The Get Right House? Have you ever tried living in a house with 5 other women *and* their kids? I'm the only one there without children. Somebody's baby is always crying, and you know how females can be. Seems like they always getting into it over nonsense. I keep to myself to avoid the drama. But they don't want none of me anyway," Nyeaylashay said with much attitude.

"So you can fight, huh?" Debra laughed thinking about her youth when she felt she could whoop any girl who stepped to her.

"When you're in a gang and the girlfriend of one of the dude's running thangs, you better know how to fight. People are always trying you to get street credibility, and other women are testing you because they want to get with your man. Sometimes you have to show'em that you ain't no punk."

"What made you decide to leave?"

Nyeaylashay took a bite of her sandwich and slowly chewed it before answering. Some of the mustard from the sandwich lodged itself in the thick gloss on her lips.

"I promised my daddy before he died that I would."

"I'm sorry to hear that. Do you mind telling me what happened?"

Nyeaylashay started looking around. "This isn't going to be on the news, is it? Where' the TV camera? My left side is my best side," she said laughing.

"Naw, I don't mind." Shay wiped her lips with her napkin. It was smeared with lip gloss, mustard, and the black pencil she used to line her lips.

"Daddy worked at night at a convenience store. One night some guys decided to rob the store and shot him in cold blood for $50 and a 40 ounce. He didn't die right away. He held on for a couple of days, but he made me promise him on his deathbed I would leave. You can't deny a dying man his last wish. But it wasn't easy. I had to leave everything. Including my boyfriend Artemis. He said he understood, but he couldn't be with me if I quit. But he was cool enough to make sure everybody knew that if something happened to me, they would have to deal with him. He'd beat them until the only way they could eat was with a feeding tube. He meant it too. So I got to leave without the drama most girls get when they try to leave."

"I'm so sorry for what happened to your father, Shay. Did they ever catch the guys who did it?" asked Debra.

Nyeaylashay's face fell into a frown. "Yep. Turned out to be two teenagers from the neighborhood. The store surveillance cameras captured their faces real good. They're both serving 30-year sentences.

"I'm glad I left the life though. It's a dead-end road. You end up dead or in jail. Artemis is the only thing I miss. He was a killer, fa sho'. But when he was with me, he was like a cute, cuddly puppy. He loved me enough to let me go. Him and my daddy wanted me to go to school and make something of myself. So that's why I'm here. I'm trying to make something of myself."

Debra moved closer to her and reached to give her a hug. Nyeaylashay started to return the hug but quickly backed away.

"Thanks but I'm cool," she said. *Tough chick* thought Debra.

"It must be hard for you, being cut off from your family and friends like that," said Debra.

"It is. I tried staying with my sister, Joy, for a while, but she's got three kids and a husband in a two-bedroom apartment. Plus, I didn't like the way her husband looked at me. It was obvious he wanted to be more than just my brother-in-law. I think Joy noticed it too. I tried living with my aunt Mabel, but she already had a house full of folks. Since I had a record, she suggested I try the Get Right program.

"I didn't want to at first, but it's not so bad. I only got another year in the program. So I have to find a way to take care of myself before I get asked to leave the house. It's sink or swim with them. They equip you with the basics and give you the tools to succeed for 2 years, and then you're on your own. I'm going to community college next semester. I enjoy school, but I can't work no regular job, Ms. Sparks. I ain't yo' average chick. I got to get a job that will make me some real money. If my daddy taught me how to do anything, he taught me the value of working hard. He was a hustler. One time he held down three jobs to take care of me and my sister after my mom died of a heart attack. I want a legal hustle this time. I don't want 5-0 always watching me. You look like you make a lot of money, Ms. Sparks. Can you help me become a top dollar news anchor like you?"

Debra looked long and hard at Nyeaylashay. That poor girl no longer had a mother or a father, and in a year she would be out on her own. She might as well be honest with her.

"Feel free to call me Debra, and I have a newsflash for you, honey. This is not a profession where you start off making a lot of money. You have to work your way up to the big bucks. When I started, I made $18,000 a year. Now they're starting reporters in the low to mid-twenties."

"Stop playing, Debra. That ain't no money. How do they expect somebody to live off that? I know you're rolling in dough. I bet you're just afraid I'll come in and steal your shine. No worries. I ain't on your level yet, but I will be. I see you on TV looking all fly and smart. I wanna be that too."

Debra smiled and took a bite of her sandwich. Nyeaylashay really didn't believe her. So many people had the misconception that she started making a lot of money from the beginning because she was on TV. They were so wrong. Her six-figure salary came with hard work and wise investments. In addition to being a news anchor, Debra also owned several commercial and residential properties. Debra thought about all those nights she spent working late in the newsroom editing stories she shot earlier in the day. She had to do it all. Set up the camera, do the interview, and then edit it. She worked hard to get where she was. As a news anchor she no longer had to chase the stories. The stories were brought to her via teleprompter, and all she did was read them. She also had to help with researching stories but she rarely reported from the field. The majority of her reporting was done from behind the desk away from the elements. In the past, she had to go out and get her stories, rain, sleet, or shine. She once had to report in the middle of a storm. The rain was beating down on her and the wind was swirling violently all around. It whipped her wet hair in her face while she nervously gripped the mic and told viewers to stay inside.

Debra thought about telling Nyeaylashay that there was no way a news station was going to hire her with all those tattoos but thought better of it. Plus, that wasn't true. Skillfully done makeup could hide just about anything. She decided that she had given Nyeaylashay enough disappointing news for one day.

Instead, she said, "Shay, everything I have came from hard work and some self-improvement. You live off meager earnings by learning to work your connections. I hosted any event I could for a fee to bring in extra income. I found a cheap apartment and learned how to budget. I cooked at home instead of eating out. I bought my clothes and shoes at consignment shops and thrift stores. I also got in good with boutique owners so they would offer me a discount or tell me when they were marking their high-end items down. If you want what I have, you have to trust me, do what I say, and follow my example. Let me ask you a question. What made you pick that outfit you have on?"

Nyeaylashay looked down at her clothes and brushed some of the crumbs from her sandwich and potato chips from her lap. "What? You don't like it? It's Baby Phat, and I look good in it. I figured you were taking me to a nice restaurant, so I needed to look nice. Is something wrong with it?" She looked herself up and down, and then looked back at Debra waiting for a response.

"That depends on your definition of good and nice. Baby Phat is cool, but I prefer to wear Kimora's KLS collection. It's a little more mature and sophisticated, but the brand name doesn't matter. Your outfit is too small, and it is highly inappropriate for a five-star restaurant. You look like you are going to some club or starring in a booty-shaking hip-hop video, not a fine dining establishment. I was almost afraid you were going to drop it low or make it clap at any minute and wait for men to make it rain. You say you want the life I lead. Have you ever seen me in anything like?"

"No. But you're older, and your job is stuffy. Someone your age would look ridiculous in something like this," said Nyeaylashay.

"Sweetheart, *you* look ridiculous," replied Debra.

Nyeaylashay was clearly offended. "Huh? *Excuse me.* I see you in your True Religion jeans and expensive blouse and matching shoes and purse, but you don't have to insult me. I have the men going crazy whenever I step outside my door. Can you say the same? *I don't think so!* You so boney. A couple of trips to the buffet would do you some good."

I like this girl. She's got some fight in her. I just have to show her how to appropriately channel it, thought Debra.

"Calm down, young lady. I haven't raised my voice at you so there is no need to raise your voice at me. And there's no need to hurl insults. I'm trying to help you. You need to learn how to take constructive criticism. First lesson of the day is dress appropriately for the occasion. You didn't see anybody in that restaurant dressed like you. Nor did I see one man breaking his neck to get near you, and if one did, he probably would have asked you if $20 was enough for your services for the evening." Debra looked at her 100% BITCH belt.

"Also, a *bitch* is a female dog. I don't care what anyone says, that's what it is, and no woman should be referred to as that. And under no circumstances should you refer to yourself as that. If you want to be respected, you should carry yourself in a manner that demands respect. If you are calling yourself out of your name, what would prevent someone else from doing it? I suggest you throw that hideously insulting belt in the trash. It serves no positive purpose. Now, finish your food, and I'll take you back to your car."

"I ain't no ho, and I ain't got no car! I rode the bus. Why you dogging me like this?" shouted Nyeaylashay.

Debra shuddered just thinking about what she must have looked like riding the bus in that get-up.

"It's *I don't have a car.* Correct English is a must in my business. Here's another lesson, Shay. If you're not selling, then why are you advertising? That outfit has *for sale at dollar store prices* written all over it. I'm not dogging you. I'm merely trying to point out the errors of your ways and the flaws in your thinking.

"I think we've both had enough for today. I'll take you back to the Get Right House." Debra began gathering her things.

Nyeaylashay was about to respond with another curt remark but stopped for a minute to think about what Debra said. True, she didn't see one person in the restaurant dressed like her. Maybe she was inappropriately dressed, but Debra didn't have to insinuate that she was a prostitute. She had always been selective about the men she slept with. Artemis was her first and only.

"Will I see you again?" she said softly.

"I'll come get you Wednesday at 3 p.m. You can sit in as I prepare to anchor the 5 p.m. broadcast, but you need to be appropriately dressed when I pick you up. You say you want to work for a news station. I want you to be dressed like a news reporter."

Nyeaylashay looked down at her lap and said, "I ain't got—I mean, I don't have dress clothes like that. I rarely have a reason to dress up."

"No worries, love. I know just the place to send you, and it won't cost you a thing," said Debra. "If you are really willing to do what I tell you without getting an attitude every time, I got you." She smiled at the young lady, who then smiled back.

The drive to the Get Right House was a quiet one. Nyeaylashay was still a little upset, but she was also afraid she would say something to make her new mentor retract her invitation for her to watch her do the news. She had never been to a television station before and could hardly contain her excitement.

After Debra pulled up in front of her group home, she reached into her purse and pulled out a small notepad and a pen, and quickly scrawled something on it.

"This is a number to Dress for Success. They give up-and-coming professionals like yourself career wear. Call the number and make an appointment. Be sure to tell them I sent you. When you're ready for a job, they can help with your interview skills as well," she said.

Nyeaylashay took the number and shoved it into her cleavage where she stowed her money, cell phone, and door key. She then sat back in the car, closed her eyes, and said, "Okay. Thanks, Debra, but can I say something without you getting mad?"

"I think I can manage that," said Debra.

Nyeaylashay opened her eyes and looked at Debra. "You hurt my feelings at the park when you said I looked like a prostitute. I've never had sex for money. Not all female gang members get passed around, and not all girls from the hood get down with any guy they meet. I really look up to you. I mean, I like watching you do the news. It hurts to know that's what you think of me. I bet you think I'm just another kid with no future like the ones you report about each night. I got dreams. I want to make something of myself."

Momma Cee's comments about her being high and mighty came flooding back to Debra. Maybe she was a bit harsh.

"I'm sorry, Shay, but I was trying to make sure I got my point across. I promise to choose my words more carefully in the future. You need to understand that your clothes can speak volumes about you before you ever open your mouth, and if you are inappropriately dressed, they may be saying the wrong thing. I can tell you're a nice young lady that got caught up with the wrong crowd. You are no longer in that environment, and if you truly want to be accepted into the world of the working professional journalist, I suggest you dress the part. Go to Dress for Success and pick yourself out a couple of nice suits for Wednesday. Keep the makeup to a minimum and find a less flamboyant hairstyle. I want you to look at as many news segments as you can between now and Wednesday and use the women you see in them as an example. Consider this your homework assignment from me.

"I'm proud of the way you just expressed yourself to me. When someone says something to you that you don't like, it's not necessary to yell and insult them. However, there is no harm in finding a tactful way to tell them how you feel. Your future is up to you. I'm glad you have goals. Now we have to formulate a plan to help you achieve them.

"I bet you didn't know that I grew up in foster care. I haven't seen my mother since I was a child, and I never knew my father. But I had a foster mother who loved me and told me that I could do anything if I was willing to put in the work. I made the decision to be successful, and you can too. I have to go now. Call me if you need me."

"Thanks, Debra". Nyeaylashay gave her a hug, exited her car, and watched her slowly drive away. She knew this was a golden opportunity, and if she played her cards right, she could make her dream of being a television news anchor come true. She was going to show Debra she had what it takes to do the news.

As Debra drove off, she made a vow to do everything within her power to help Nyeaylashay leave the life she fled behind for good. She needed a good female role model with some connections to help her stay on the right track, and that's exactly what she was going to get. Momma Cee was right. It was high time she gave her time to someone besides herself.

Success Is the Best Revenge

Do not take revenge, my friends, but leave room for God's wrath, for it is written: "It is mine to avenge: I will repay," says the Lord.
—Romans 12:19

Janice clutched the letter in her pocket tightly. Her palms were so sweaty that the blue ink on the paper began to smear. It only contained a few nondescriptive lines, but it was what the letter didn't say that made it so intriguing.

She was in the living room helping her favorite aunt mend her uncle's work clothes when the postman came to deliver the certified letter. Janice wondered how the writer found her. She didn't tell anyone where she was going. After the scandal, as she referred to it, and her separation from her husband, John, she disappeared. She knew that no one would think to look for her on her aunt and uncle's small farm in Oklahoma. Not even her husband, since he always thought he was too good to come visit her family "in the country" when they were together. Her mother was the only person who knew of her whereabouts, and Janice knew that she would never rat her out.

She was curious to know who wrote the letter and what it meant. The words scrawled in tiny neat script read, *How would you like your old life back? You once extended me your friendship when I needed it most. Please allow me to return the favor. Meet me tomorrow for dinner at 6 p.m.*

It was followed by the name and address of one of the most popular diners in the town, Lucille's.

Janice arrived 15 minutes early because she wanted to beat the crowd and get a good view of the man or woman who thought they could restore her life as soon as he or she entered. She opened the door to the eatery to find Lucille herself serving as hostess. This was rare since the old woman retired about 3 years ago and left the daily operation to her only son, Clive. She joined a senior's travel group and was always on some cruise or exploring what she called "new territory". But every now and then when she began to miss the hustle and bustle of her busy diner and her favorite customers, Lucille came to her namesake place and behaved as if she'd never left. Lucille was fond of Janice. As a child, she spent her summers in Oklahoma and her uncle and aunt would bring her to the restaurant once a week for some homemade vanilla ice cream and a slice of apple pie. Lucille would always make sure she got a nice portion of crust just the way Janice liked it.

"Hey, Suga Dumpling! Gon' head and find you a seat and I'll send somebody over to take your order," Lucille called out.

"Take your time, Ms. Lou. I'm expecting a guest and he hasn't arrived yet."

"He?" Lucille asked while peering over her brown horn-rimmed spectacles with a raised eyebrow. "It better not be that no-count husband of yours, or I'm gone do like Savannah did in *Waiting to Exhale* and pour water all in his lap."

Word got around the town pretty quickly that she was on her way to divorce court. Most of the people in the town only knew bits and pieces of what happened, but to them, Janice was like family. They watched her grow up. She played with their children, spent the night during sleepovers, ate dinner at their tables, and worshipped with them on Sundays. The worst thing you can do is mess with family. John was on the hit list of several people he never met and didn't know existed.

"No worries, Ms. Lou. To tell you the truth it might be a she. You can save the water for your customers," she smiled.

Janice sat down, picked up a menu, and looked at it as if she didn't already know everything that was on it. She held out her hands and examined her semi-dirty unmanicured nails.

It was mind-boggling how her life had changed in a matter of weeks. One of the highlights of her week used to be her trips to the spa. She could no longer afford her massage, facial, manicure, and pedicure appointments. Even if she could, it wouldn't be practical when you live and work on a farm. Getting your hands dirty was part of the job requirements. Cooking, cleaning, laundry, and helping her uncle prepare the fields for planting were all in a day's work. Each evening before dinner she scrubbed the thick rich dark earth from beneath her fingernails. Sometimes she had to wash them at least three times to get it all out. Her manicure and polish wouldn't last 2 days under those conditions.

Janice laughed, but it wasn't a laugh of joy. It was the laugh someone gives when they are walking that thin line between sanity and insanity. Everything she held dear was ripped away from her simply because she did what she had to do to give her conscience peace. It tormented her day and night as she fought to convince herself that it was okay not to turn the information she knew over to the proper authorities. She talked it over with her husband, and he told her that if she did that, she would not only ruin their lives but hundreds of others as well.

"Some things are better left unsaid," he stated. But she couldn't. As an environmental specialist she knew that the toxins her company was allowing to seep into the water table and the soil were hazardous and could lead to severe illness and possibly even the deaths of the people in the small neighboring town. She and most of the people who worked at the plant didn't live there. The town was small and poor, and plant employees, most of who made an above-average salary, could afford to live in more affluent areas. So they did. Some drove an hour or more to and from work.

Janice enjoyed her job at Valcrex, and she was good at it. When she noticed the company was growing lax in their hazardous waste disposal standards, she tried to alert her bosses to the problem. She soon learned that they were "trying something new" to save money and told her that she needn't worry herself about it. She begged them to do the right thing and bring in the equipment to properly dispose of the hazardous manufacturing by-products they made during production each day. Upper management told her that they would look into it, but the necessary equipment cost millions, and it would take time to get it. They tried to pacify her with a month's paid vacation and a bonus. She was told when she got back everything would be up to code. Janice wanted to stay and supervise the changes, but they told her that wasn't necessary. She reluctantly took her month's leave and spent the time relaxing and bonding with her children. She even when to the Virgin Islands for a week.

When she returned to work, she realized that the toxins being re-leased into the environment were worse than ever. Nothing had changed. Janice refused to eat at the local restaurants for fear that they were cooking the food from water found in the nearby reservoir. Each day she brought lunch for her and her husband, who also worked for the company. She encouraged her coworkers to do the same. She tried to appeal to her bosses again, but she was told that if she wanted to keep her job she better keep quiet. That silenced her for a little while. She had grown accustomed to her life of luxury and had no desire to give it up. But at what cost?

The guilt Janice felt became unbearable. She was tormented day and night by the dirty secret she was being forced to carry. She couldn't eat. She couldn't sleep. She tried to keep busy so she wouldn't think about the toxins poisoning those in the town, but there wasn't enough work to be done to make her forget Valcrex's dastard-ly deed. Then one day she couldn't continue to stand under the weight of her guilt any longer and called the Environmental Protection Agency. She even sent them documentation to corroborate her claims. She felt better but wondered what would happen next. She didn't have to wonder long because within a week, the place was swarming with investigators.

The EPA closed the plant, and it stayed closed for over a month. During that time, the board of directors disavowed any wrongdoing and fired all the heads of the company, making it seem as if they were operating independently. They even fired the founder's son, Mitchell Valcrex, Jr. They brought in new people and began a neighborhood cleanup campaign. Fines were levied and paid, and it appeared that things were going well and the company was slated to reopen. Alt-hough, Janice and her husband were not among those employees asked to return. Their positions were given to others.

The company looked like it was going to recover from the scandal until the residents of the town filed a multi-million dollar lawsuit. Valcrex was being accused of being responsible for the scores of people being diagnosed with cancer, multiple miscarriages among the women, and three deaths. The two sides couldn't reach an amicable settlement so the case went to trial. After listening to scientific testimony that clearly concluded that the toxins released by Valcrex were responsible for the town's ill population, the judge decided to make an example out of them and awarded the town and its people $500 million. The company had no choice but to file bankruptcy and close its doors forever.

Valcrex wasn't the only thing in shambles. So was Janice's life. Janice was labeled a whistle-blower and blackballed within the manufacturing industry. Everyone in her company hated her because in their eyes, her honesty had stripped them of their lucrative salaries and the posh lifestyles that came with them. They were all simultaneously thrust into unemployment.

John was resentful as well. He didn't see why she couldn't keep her mouth shut and continue to pack their lunches every day. At least until the two of them had devised a plan to leave the company with their careers and bank accounts still intact. Living 8 months without any income ravaged their bank accounts and 401k. They had a hefty mortgage, two luxury vehicles, and their children were enrolled in private school. John said he felt like she betrayed him. She shouldn't have made that phone call without consulting him first, and the fact that she did showed that she didn't care enough to put their family first. He said she jeopardized their lives and their livelihood. In a way, he was right. In addition to losing their lucrative jobs, for months they received hate mail and phone calls at home and on their cell phones from angry former coworkers who thought she should have kept her mouth shut, too. It amazed Janice how they had no compassion for the men, women, and children they were poisoning each day.

John was able to find a job in Chicago. After he made that announcement, he stated that he wanted a divorce. Janice wasn't surprised. Twenty years of marriage had dwindled to this. All they did was fight, and they hadn't touched each other in months. They gave their 3 kids the option to choose which parent they wanted to live with. Had things been different she would have fought for full-custody but Janice was tired and she had no money to take care of them, anyway. She also believed that her husband's parenting skills were every bit as good as her own. The eldest, Joseph, followed the money. He was a spoiled, selfish 14-year-old who was used to the best of everything. He did not enjoy the lean months the family experienced and was elated about the opportunity to be rid of them. His 7-year-old little brother, Westin, who mimicked everything

Joseph did, followed suit. He said he couldn't see life without his big brother.

However, their sweet 12-year-old daughter, Adaline, stayed loyal to her mother and remained under her charge. She followed her to Oklahoma without a single complaint. It was obvious that she missed her suburban lifestyle with destination play dates and spa parties at shops that specifically catered to kids, but she took it in stride and adapted to the slower-paced country life that was now her own.

Janice was grateful for the kindness of family. Her uncle and aunt welcomed her with open arms and told her that she could stay as long as she needed. Janice was flat broke except for the money she received from pawning her wedding ring and other expensive jewelry. Her degree in biology did little for her in her new surroundings.

As she sat there waiting, she questioned her decision. She used to think making that phone call was the right thing to do, but sitting there in jeans, a flannel shirt, with hair that desperately needed a few hours at a good beauty salon, and unmanicured hands with broken nails made her begin to think otherwise.

"Hello, Janice," a soft voice that she instantly recognized said from behind her.

She swung around to face Mr. Willie Arnold. He served as the CFO of Valcrex for over 20 years until they fired him. He was a sweet soul who believed in investing in the lives of others. When the company was booming, he presented a proposal to the board to increase the benefits of the employees that included more insurance and 401k contributions from the company. He wanted to put a day care onsite and start a job training program to allow more people from the town to qualify for the more technical positions within the company. He also wanted to implement tuition reimbursement and a bunch of other programs that companies that appear on the "Best Places to Work" lists each year do for their employees.

Willie was soon released from his position. The leadership at Valcrex was about making money, not spending money. His business savvy helped make that company profitable, and they fired him because he wanted to give back to the men and women who helped Valcrex to excel. It was sad. Willie looked so dejected when they gave him his walking papers. Janice saw him being escorted out of the building by security as if he stole something. As he stood by his car fumbling with his keys, she asked him to join her for a cup of coffee. He accepted. They went to one of the town restaurants and talked about everything but work. She even got him to smile and laugh a couple of times before they said good-bye.

Janice recalled that her last words to him were, "This job doesn't determine your outcome. You do."

Willie smiled, gave her a hug and a peck on the cheek, and said, "Thank you, dear." He then got in his BMW and drove away. Janice never heard or saw Willie again, until now.

She stood, and he gave her a tight embrace. He looked like he was doing well. Of course, he had aged a little over the years, but so had Janice. He was smartly dressed in a blue tailored suit, but there was something else different about him. Willie had a sparkle in his eye that hadn't been there before. It was the look of a man who found his purpose in life and was happy.

"Sit, sit, sit," he said. Willie took off his hat and suit coat and had a seat. "You were not an easy lady to find. I had to hire a private investigator. My investigator couldn't get a thing out of your mother. Your ex-husband doesn't even know where you are."

Janice laughed. "I know. I was afraid the evil bastard would try to ask me for child support so I won't give him an address, but I do call and talk to my sons at least twice a week. I was hoping to go visit them in a month or two. My mother said someone came to see her, but she couldn't remember who it was. She's pretty good at keeping a secret."

Willie nodded. "That she is. Don't worry, I won't tell John where you are. You've been through a lot. It isn't easy picking up the pieces of your life, is it?"

"What life?" said Janice. "I feed chickens, slop hogs, till soil, and milk cows all day."

"Yet, you're alive to do it, and that's what matters. Every day you are above ground is a gift. Don't you go getting all bitter and angry. It achieves nothing. Believe me, I know. Besides, I've come to save you."

Janice was glad that he got straight to the point. "Save me? How?" she asked.

"Didn't I say it in my note? I'm here to give you your life back, or at least the quality of life you once had. I've been very busy since I left Valcrex. I am now the president of a small but expensive private college in upstate New York. I've been looking at ways to enhance our business program. It's successful in its own right, but I know we can make it better. What I've come up with is a curriculum focused not only on the fundamental principles of business but ethics.

"America has become too selfish. Too many businesses are more concerned about their bottom line than they are for the people who work for them. Charity is done to get tax breaks, not because they really want to help people. This mentality has created men and women with no loyalty to the companies they serve. That's why turnover is so high. Employees stay long enough to acquire new skills, and then they take them to the competition. For an employer, that can be nerve-wracking because as soon as you have a solid worker who knows his or her position and how to excel at it, you lose them. Then you have to bring someone new in and train them all over again. You could bring in someone who already has the skills, but that can become expensive. Top-notch talent commands high salaries. But there is more to it than that." He furrowed has brow before he continued.

"I watch these kids we graduate with honors every year, and they are ruthless. They'd rather work hard at trying to throw their coworkers under the bus than they would at excelling at their own jobs. It's every person for themselves. We have some of the most brilliant minds at our university, but their morals concern me. We need more men and women with good ethics in business, and that is why I've been combing the earth looking for you, my dear Janice."

Janice wasn't sure how she fit into all of this. He needed to make his intentions plainer. "What exactly do you have in mind?"

"I want you to head the department," Willie said matter-of-factly.

"But I don't know the first thing about business. I'm a biologist."

"I know that, but you can learn. Do you still have that recipe for those delicious cookies you used to bring to the office?"

Janice wished he would stick to the subject. She wanted to talk about her future, not cookies. "My Grandma Addie's butter pecan cookies?" she asked.

"Yes. Those were delicious," the old man licked his lips as if he were tasting one at that very moment.

"Of course, I do. My kids love them."

"As they should. They were the most delectable treats I have ever eaten, and I've eaten a lot of food in my day." Willie rubbed his Santa Claus-like stomach.

"I always thought that if you ever marketed those they would be a hit. It's high time you did. I'm prepared to give you the seed money and the connections to launch your own cookie business. I'm not just talking any cookie business, either. I'm talking about along the lines of Mrs. Fields, Little Debbie, Hostess, Famous Amos. I can't present you as the best thing to ever happen to my school if you don't have the business credentials to back it up. You've got the right moral compass, but I need more."

Janice sat quietly letting it all sink in. During that time Megean, Lucille's niece, came over and took their orders.

Several minutes after she left their table Janice said, "Why would you do this for me?"

"Number one, I hate to see a good person knocked down and dragged through the dirt. You did the right thing, Janice. Don't you doubt your decision to alert the authorities to that sludge they were pumping in the water supply for one minute."

"But that decision cost me everything—my marriage, my sons, my job, even my career. No one will hire me. They're all afraid I'm a snitch. How do you hold your head up high when you go from living in a $300,000 house in the land of the affluent and influential to a small-town farmhouse in a place most of the world doesn't even know exists?"

"You hold your head up high because you are a child of God, and as such, you are royalty. God Himself said that you are the head, not the tail, and your enemies shall be your footstool. Would it make you feel any better if I told you that you would still have lost it if you kept you mouth closed?" Willie looked at her slyly as if he had a secret. Meagan returned with one hot tea and an orange soda. Janice waited until she left to respond.

"What do you mean?"

Willie spoke slowly and softly. "Exactly what I said. Valcrex was getting ready to ruin your career by making it seem as if you were the one turning your head to those environmental violations and falsifying documents. You were going to take the fall for those toxins seeping into the environment and you probably would have ended up in jail. You foiled those plans by contacting the authorities first."

"What?" Janice slammed her fist on the table shaking their beverages. "How do you know that?"

"I have my sources. You can't work for a company as long as I did and not make a few friends. That 1-month vacation they gave you was so they could alter documents, falsify water and soil tests, and the like. They were going to run you over with a Mack truck, and then leave your carcass lying there so the vultures could pick what was left off your bones. It would have been the scandal of the century. And as for that husband of yours, he was in on the plan. They offered him a lot of money to keep them abreast of your every move. Why do you think he was so upset when you called the EPA without telling him first? He wanted to be rich beyond his wildest dreams more than he wanted his wife."

Janice felt a wave of heat wash over her. Her face was flushed, and she was sweating bullets. Her flannel shirt instantly felt like a thick blanket against her skin. She reached for the glass of cold orange soda in front of her and took several large gulps.

The old man chuckled. "I want you to get angry, Janice. Angry enough to do the hard work it takes for you to regain your rightful position in life. A good woman like you should be on top," said Willie.

"I'm going to kill him," growled Janice. "Here I was thinking I killed my marriage, and he was already doing so in order to line his pockets." She stood to leave. She needed to get to Chicago, slap her husband, and get her sons.

"Sit down, Janice," Willie said calmly, and then took a sip of his tea. "Doing something rash will only make matters worse. Didn't you say that you have a daughter to take care of? What will happen to her if you end up in the penitentiary?"

The mere thought of her sweet loyal Adaline made Janice settle back into her chair. She was named after the woman who helped raised Janice, her deceased grandmother Addie. Janice had to make sure that she was taken care of at all costs. As far as she was concerned, the child was all she had left.

"I am offering you a fool proof plan to enact the best kind of revenge there is . . . success. All your haters, as the kids say, will be green with envy. What do you think John and those money-grubbing leeches you used to work for will say when they see you as the head of a multi-million dollar company and the head of a successful business ethics program at a prestigious school?"

That brought a twisted smile to Janice's face, but she was still skeptical. Was Willie secretly one of those heartless vultures she used to work for? Was she about to sell her soul to the devil?

"Why me? What do you get out of this?" she asked.

"I get to go down in history as one of the smartest college presidents who ever lived. Who better to head an ethics program than a whistle-blower? You risked everything to save a few hundred people in a measly little town no one seemed to care about. If this program is successful, we'll be able to compete with all the ivy leagues— Harvard, Yale, Stanford."

Willie's eyes glistened as the names rolled off his tongue. Then his tone softened, and he looked down at the table.

"I also get the pleasure of thanking a woman who prevented an old man from going home and committing suicide many years ago. That company was everything to me. I gave Valcrex 20 years of my life. My best friend and I made that company great, but after he died, that dunce son of his took over and forgot everything his father stood for. Mitchell Valcrex was a brilliant man of integrity and valor. That plan I presented to the board was all the things Mitchell said he wanted to do for his employees once the company reached a certain level of financial success. I was hoping to honor a dead man's wishes. But it wasn't to be. At least not at Valcrex. I felt like I had let Mitchell down when the board rejected my proposal. I was planning to revise it and give it another shot, but they fired me a week later. I have no wife and no kids. That job was everything to me. The people working there were my family, and they were stripped away from me over a difference in opinion.

"You know I had enough knowledge of dirty little secrets to ruin just about every man and woman on that board of directors and in the executive offices. You learn quite a bit when you keep quiet and observe. I knew who was sleeping with whom, who was using company credit cards for personal expenses, who was hiding company funds from the IRS."

"Why didn't you use that information for your benefit?" asked Janice. "I would have."

"That would have made me no better than them. I've been around long enough to know that when you seek to put someone in their grave, make sure you dig a second one for yourself. Karma has a way of getting you too when evil is your motivation. I prefer to keep love in my heart and let God handle my enemies. Revenge is mine saith the Lord!

"I loved Valcrex, but the company was changing. Junior was systematically ruining the wonderful office culture his father managed with respect and concern for the well-being of his employees. Junior believed in fear, intimidation, and getting the most out of people for the least amount of money. Greed was his downfall."

Willie looked a little teary eyed for a moment, but then he shook his head, smiled, and said, "So, are you in or out?"

Janice smiled. She had no idea Willie remembered their talk over coffee so fondly. She wondered if he really would have killed himself or was he exaggerating. Besides, he seemed sincere. What did she have to lose?

"I'm in," she said. "The good thing about being at the bottom is the only place you can go is up."

Willie shook his head. "No, that's the wrong attitude. God needed to put you in a new position so that you could grow. You were a potted plant at Valcrex and your roots had reached the bottom of the pot. Now, you're in rich, deep soil, and your roots can grow in any direction and receive all the nutrients they need."

Willie took a final sip of his tea, and then grabbed his coat and hat. "Now that we have come to an agreement, I must be going. A food chemist is going to be at your house tomorrow at 2 p.m. Show him your recipe so that he can figure out the best ingredients to keep your cookies fresh on the shelves without compromising their flavor. Then, you'll meet your business coach, and she will show you how to launch and create a successful business.

"I truly can't thank you enough for what you did that day. All these years you thought you merely bought an old man a cup of coffee. You did much more than that. You lit a spark that turned into a raging fire. I took that fire to where it was needed. A college that was looking for someone who knew numbers and was up to the challenge of saving a fledgling institution from going bankrupt. I did that, and now I head the college and can hire anyone I want if they have the right credentials. And I want you. Remember, dear, that job doesn't determine your outcome, you do. Forget that no-good husband of yours and let's go make history."

Janice stood and shook his hand. Willie took a step toward the door and stopped, "Oh, I almost forgot," he said as he reached under his coat and pulled out a large bulky manila envelope and handed it to her.

She turned it over, but there was nothing written on it to indicate its contents.

"What's this?" she asked.

"Thank-you letters from the townspeople you saved from years of severe health calamities. Every time you start to doubt that you did the right thing by calling the EPA, you pull out a letter and read it. There's a real tearjerker in there from a mother of three named Pearl. She was able to use the money she got from Valcrex to pay for her husband's cancer treatments. He would have died without them.

"Get ready to be rich beyond your wildest dreams, dear. I trust you won't let it go to your head. I'll see you soon."

He kissed her cheek and headed toward the door.

Epilogue

Willie kept his promise and made Janice rich beyond her wildest dreams. Her finances and her personal life were changed forever. Janice fell in love with the food chemist Willie sent to her house to help her with her cookie recipe. Together, with the help of the business coach and Willie's financial backing, they founded Victory Foods and introduced the world to Grandma Addie's Butter Pecan Cookies. They later launched an entire catalogue of cookies, cakes, pies, and candies. Victory Foods was named one of America's fastest-growing companies after it grossed over $1 million in 2 years. Janice worked hard for every dime the company earned. The crash course in business she received was lucrative but tiring. Willie refused to help her run it, but he did offer advice whenever asked. The only way she was going to be qualified to head an entire department in his college was to succeed at running a business and learn for herself the lessons that came with it.

Willie also became like a father to Janice and a grandfather to Adaline, who affectionately referred to him as Paw Paw. Willie became richer than he had ever been before, too. The love of a family that he lacked for years was provided by simply helping a woman who did the same for him. His share of the profits from Janice's company didn't hurt either.

Janice gladly divorced John and remarried. After 2 years, her new husband, whose name was Luke, took over the daily operations of the company so Janice could return to school to obtain her Ph.D. Willie arranged for her to take an accelerated 1-year program. Upon graduation, she took over as chair of the business department of Oberlin Brown College. She worked hard to create a program built on a foundation of ethics as Willie asked. She also became a highly sought after public speaker and frequently attended company conferences and presented the topic of how to implement ethical practices into the workplace.

As for Janice's ex-husband, John married a cute little secretary in his office named Kristin but found out the hard way the she was only with him for his money. When the recession hit and he lost his job, she ran off with a millionaire she met on Richgentlemen.com, but not before she cleaned out John's bank account and left him with the infant daughter they had together. He was now an unemployed, impoverished single father of three. His only saving grace was the child support Janice agreed to pay each month. It kept them afloat until he was able to find another job. Although it came too late for their eldest son, Joseph. After his father lost his job, Joseph and some friends robbed a liquor store and accidently shot and killed the clerk that tried to stop them. When the police asked him why he did it, the 18-year-old high school senior confessed that he was trying to score enough cash to get the new iPhone his father could no longer afford to buy him. He was sentenced to 15 years. His mother puts money on his books every month so he can get all the chips, cookies, and Jungle Juice he wants. His favorite snack is Grandma Addie's Butter Pecan Cookies.

You Reap What You Sow

Do not be deceived. God cannot be mocked. A man reaps what he sows. The one who sows to please his sinful nature, from that nature will reap destruction; the one who sows to please the Spirit, from the Spirit will reap eternal life. Let us not become weary of doing good, for at the proper time we will reap a harvest if we do not give up.
—Galatians 6:7–9

I love to lie in bed and watch him as he quietly slips his clothes on. His body is toned and taut for a 45-year-old man. I run my hand over the golden brown skin on his back. He looks back at me and smiles. At times like this, it's easy to pretend that he belongs to me.

"I was trying not to wake you," he said.

I yawned and said drowsily, "You did a horrible job. It's that time already? Will I see you tomorrow?"

He turned and looked at me again. "I doubt it. Tomorrow is my wife's birthday, and we're throwing her a birthday party. We usually spend the entire day together afterward. Those things can be so exhausting. My wife knows anyone who's anyone in Chicago and we spend half the night laughing at the stale jokes of dignitaries and smiling at people who know us, but we have no idea who they are."

Ouch! I received a sharp dose of reality in the form of a simple answer to a simple question. I'd been sharing Oscar Pendleton for 3 years. I have him, at least twice a week; if I'm lucky 3 times, but he always leaves and goes back to her. I never meant to become involved with a married man, but he came along at a time when I really needed someone. He was my knight in shining armor who slayed the dragons of deferred dreams, poverty, and homelessness.

It wasn't always this way. I met Oscar when I was 18. I had just graduated from high school and was looking forward to college. But my bright future was almost shattered when my crackhead mother threw me out of the house because I wouldn't give her any money to buy drugs. Determined not to let it deter me, I took my meager belongings and went to the church my Grams attended for over 50 years for help. The church always seemed to be her place of refuge in times of storms. Maybe it could be mine, too. They directed me to a homeless shelter for women. The women who ran the shelter were nice. They encouraged me to excel in spite of my circumstances and helped me land a job at Burger Barn as a cashier. They saw potential in me and allowed me to stay at the shelter longer than most residents were allowed to in order to save money for college during the summer. I was accepted to the University of Illinois at Chicago, better known as UIC, and was scheduled to begin in the fall but financial aid did not cover all of my expenses.

A few weeks later, my mother died of a drug overdose. I was so distraught that I couldn't even bring myself to arrange the funeral. My aunt handled all the arrangements.

It wasn't the best of circumstances but at least I wasn't on the street. I ate three meals a day, and I was employed. I had a plan, and I was determined to work it and create a brighter future for myself.

Each day during my break I would take a bun or two and go feed the birds in a nearby park. Ever since I was a child I loved the park. There was just something about this little piece of nature nestled within the hustle and bustle of a busy city that always intrigued me.

One day while sitting on a bench people watching, I met Oscar. His demeanor was very warm, and he asked me questions as if he were genuinely interested in who I was and what I was doing with my life. Before I knew it I had given him the condensed version of my pitiful life. He told me that I was a strong young lady and left.

I began seeing him in the park more frequently, and each time he was full of encouraging words. In the beginning, Oscar was just a friend and made no advances toward me. He told me I reminded him of his baby sister and because of that, he felt a certain connection between the two of us. The day I told him I got promoted to shift leader at my job he insisted that I come to his house and eat dinner with his family to celebrate. He said he told them all about me and wanted us to meet. I agreed. After work, he picked me up in his

Escalade, took me to the shelter, and waited patiently as I showered and changed clothes.

I had no idea that Oscar was loaded until I saw his home. He lived in a massive house right off the lake in the south loop of Chicago. I'd seen these houses as I drove through the neighborhood with friends or family, but I'd never been in one. Everything in it screamed luxury and expensive. I saw paintings that looked like they should have been in a museum and furniture that looked too nice to sit on. I was afraid to touch anything because I knew if I broke something I wouldn't be able to pay for it. That night I met his beautiful wife, Vivian. She was intelligent, refined, and witty. It was easy to see why he married her. I also met their two adolescent children, Maxwell and Miranda.

Oscar and his family were really nice to me. They made me feel special. Oscar even had their cook make my favorite dish, lasagna, and bake a special cake with the word *Congratulations* in colorful letters. That was the first of several nights I spent with Oscar and his family. Although, most of the time it was just me and his kids. I always enjoyed when Vivian was able to join us, but as a senior partner in a law firm, she worked long hours and rarely made it home in time for dinner.

What I loved most about Oscar was that he listened. I really needed someone at that point in my life. When your own mother puts you out, and then dies of a drug overdose, you feel unwanted with a deep sense of abandonment. It was as if I had no value. I had family other than my mother, but they had their own problems and didn't want or need to be burdened down with mine. From the day I met him, Oscar made me feel like I was someone special and I had something to contribute to those around me. I told him my dreams for my future and over time, he became a part of them.

I've always been a good student, and math is my favorite subject. I knew that education was my way out of the life of poverty I was born into. But I was afraid that my financial aid wouldn't be enough to cover the cost of everything. I shared my fears with Oscar. He told me not to worry, the UI was his and his wife's alma mater, and they were active alumni. He pulled some strings to get me accepted on a partial scholarship. The scholarship, along with my financial aid, was enough to pay for tuition and books. All I had to do was continue to work in order to pay my housing and living expenses.

I started college that fall and loved every minute of it. I loved my campus, my classes, and my professors. I loved the opportunity to learn new things. Oscar called me every week to check on me. It was almost like having a father for the first time in my life. I never knew my biological father because my mother said she didn't know who he was.

It was hard working 30 or more hours a week and going to school, but I was determined to succeed. I was driven, which left little free time. The girls in my dorm were always telling me that I worked too hard and needed to have some fun, but who had time for fun? I was a woman on a mission.

Having Oscar in my life worked wonders for my self-esteem. He told me I was attractive and smart and that I could succeed if I had a plan and worked hard. He challenged me to always do my best. He once told me that mediocrity and "good enough" were for losers. If I ever wanted to make something of myself I had to strive to be the best. That stuck with me and motivated me to study hard, and it paid off. Each semester I made the dean's list. It seemed like things were finally falling into place. I had a job, a place to lay my head, and someone who cared about me.

One day after an extremely tiring shift at the Burger Barn I was informed by my manager they were letting me go because of budget cuts. I was mortified! I needed that money to pay my bills! I called Oscar hysterical. The next installment of my dorm fees was due in 2 weeks, and I wasn't going to be able to pay it without that money. He came and picked me up from work and took me to the park where we met. I sat in his truck and wailed on his shoulder. He pulled out his handkerchief, dried my tears, and handed me $500. He assured me that everything was going to be all right and that he was there for me. Somehow his words soothed me and relief replaced my anguish. At that moment I knew that he was capable of making all my problems go away. I was grateful that he was willing to do so.

As I sat looking at him with tears of gratitude glistening on my face, he reached over, gently lifted my chin upward, and kissed me. I was stunned. Oscar was like a father to me, and you don't lock lips with your father. His warm tongue softly made its way around my moist mouth. My shock faded, and I felt a wave of emotion I never felt before. The kiss grew deeper and more intimate with every second. I'd never had a man who truly cared about me show me this type of affection. In high school the boys only wanted sex and would tell me any lie they thought I wanted to hear in order to get it. The men my mother brought home never seemed to care much for me either. They were mean to me or they wanted to sleep with me too. No one had taken a romantic interest in me for quite some time, but that was probably my fault. There was no shortage of men on campus, but I was so busy with class and work I ignored every man that wasn't one of my professors. That kiss was different from any I had ever encountered. It was more than foreplay. That kiss held passion and meaning, and I wanted more.

Oscar's hands began to move along the curves of my body, and I made no attempt to stop him. I was yearning for physical touch, affection, someone to fill the space in me that had always been void. That evening, Oscar and I made love in his SUV. It was less than ideal accommodations, but believe me when I say it was the best I ever had. And it only got better.

Oscar and I began having sex as often as our schedules would allow. I had experienced sex before, but what we did was on a different level. My past partners were little boys compared to him. This was a full-fledged man, and he knew how to treat a woman. I loved the way Oscar adored me and my body. I stood a petite 5 foot 2, and my body had more curves than a Hot Wheels track. I had cocoa-butter hips, thighs, booty, and breasts at my disposal to tease or please with it at will. I became Oscar's secret lover, and I loved it! My greatest joy was no longer excelling in school. It was pleasing him, whether it was by preparing a delicious meal, sharing a new intellectual fact, or a new lovemaking position.

A month after our love affair began, Oscar moved me off campus and into my own condo so we could stop meeting at hotels and have some privacy. But this wasn't just any condo. This was a condo in downtown Chicago with an amazing view of the harbor. It was also within walking distance of his office, and he came by often to fulfill his appetite for me. The condo was the first of many expensive gifts I received from Oscar. He paid all my bills, and he bought me a BMW so I wouldn't have to take public transportation unless I wanted to. I was used to it, but who cared? I was 19 with a Beamer! He told me I no longer had to work and gave me a monthly allowance of $1,000 a month to spend on myself. So, you know I was rockin' Dolce & Gabbana, Fendi, Hermès, Baby Phat, Chloé, and all that other fly gear. I started getting my hair and nails done every week too. Before, I did my perm at home and only got my nails done as a special treat.

Oscar took good care of me and for the first time in my life I was in love. But I couldn't enjoy it, not completely. I often felt bad because he was somebody else's husband, and I wished every day he was mine.

Once I confided my love affair guilt to my older cousin Boosie. He laughed and said, "Yo, my lil' cuz done got her a sugar daddy. Don't surprise me all that back you got. I always know'd you was gon' let somebody start tappin' that sooner or later. Glad you had some sense to get somebody with some ends. Don't worry about that fool's wife. You ain't the one that's married. So, you ain't doing nothin' wrong. You just get yours. You let him pay for all your bills and all your schoolin', get a good job, and when you get tired of old dude, dump him. Me and you, we came from the same thing, cuz . . . nothing. Now you got something. You wanna go back to nothin'?"

I shook my head no.

"I didn't think so. Moms worked three jobs to support us after my trifling daddy left. Now, look at her. Best woman I know is 40 and looks 60. She's tired, Mel. She's run-down, broke, busted, and disgusted. Worked all them years and ain't got nothing but three kids and scars to show for it. That's why I'm in dez streets hustlin'. I'ma get her outta the hood if it's the last thing I do. I owe her that much.

"I know Grams took you to church and everything, and she the reason you feelin' guilty now. That's why you and yo' moms couldn't get along. She said she felt like you thought you was better than her and was judging her and looking down on her. She was doing the best she could, but she just couldn't let go of that pipe. But where was God when she put you out? Where was He when she let them men she brought home beat you and treat you like you wasn't supposed to be in your own house? So, this what you do every time your conscience gets to botherin' you about doin' a married man. You look at this plush pad you got and then go get in your BMW and go to the Gucci store and buy yourself something expensive. I bet your conscience will shut up then!" he laughed again, showing the four gold teeth at the top of his mouth. Then he got real serious and dropped his voice low. "The best thing you can do is convince him to leave his wife for you. Then you can have it all, and your conscience will be quiet for good."

I decided that wasn't such a bad idea. I was his wife when she wasn't around anyway. The next night after making love I mentioned to Oscar the prospect of making me his number one. The answer he gave me let me know exactly where I stood.

"I think you're confused, Melanie, so listen to me carefully. I love you, but I'm not going to lose my life for you or any other woman. My wife and I got married young, so there's no prenup. We have cash, stocks, property, cars, and kids together, but most of all, we've got history. I live a comfortable life, and I like it that way.

"Vivian may be busy, but she's still the first woman I ever loved, and I can't see my life without her. Besides, we have kids, and I would never make them watch their family dissolve in front of them. So, if your plan is to get me to leave my wife, forget it. Relax and enjoy what we have. I take good care of you, and there's room for both of you in my life. A lot of women would kill to have what you have, so don't go messing it up with white dress dreams."

That should have been my wake-up call, but I couldn't bear to think of life without Oscar. I knew our relationship wasn't just about sex. It was obvious that I provided the love and attention that he didn't get at home. In return, he showed his gratitude monetarily, emotionally, and physically. Vivian didn't realize how good she had it. She had an intelligent, handsome, hardworking man to come home to every day, and she'd rather stay at work until 9 or 10 p.m. almost every night. Was she stupid?

Oscar said he always knew his wife was a workaholic, but he thought she would slow down when they had kids. Instead, she hired a maid and a nanny and went right back to work.

When Oscar and I first met, I used to hang out with the kids from time to time. They were pretty cool, but when he and I started sleeping together, he didn't want me having a close relationship with his family any longer. I didn't mind because I no longer wanted to enter his home. I hated looking at their family portraits. It made me feel sick to my stomach when I saw all the things I wanted but couldn't have. Oscar takes care of me, but his wife gets what I get times 2. I don't understand how she didn't see that her career aspirations were leaving the door wide open for another woman to sample that good thing of hers.

I once asked him if he'd tried to talk to her about it and he responded in an exasperated tone, "Several times, but I realized that being a high-powered attorney is how she identifies herself. It's an adrenaline rush for her. I think if she stopped working she would feel like less of a person. My wife needs status to validate who she is, but I'm just the opposite. I take more pride in being a devoted husband and father then I ever did in being a CPA. I'm the third-highest-ranked investment banker at an institution that's valued at millions. Now that I've achieved status, power, and money, I want to relax and have some fun. The problem was that I had no one to have fun with until you came along. I am grateful for you, Melanie. You have no idea how grateful."

My heart melted at that moment, and he's right. We have sooooo much fun together, and I'm doing things I thought I would never do. Oscar expanded my horizons. He took me to my first play, my first symphony, and my first elegant restaurant where I sampled gourmet cuisine. I was amazed to see that people would pay such high prices for so little food. Back in the day when Grams sold plate lunches, you could get a plate full of food with chicken, greens, yams, and spaghetti, sweet tea *and* a slice of pound cake for dessert, all for $8.

Oscar also took me to museums and art galleries, and I loved when we would go out of town. We rode in limousines, stayed at five-star hotels, had spa treatments—the works. It's nice to see how the other half lives. But the best part of our out-of-town trips was that I had Oscar all to myself. No wife and no kids to go home to. I got to wake up next to the man I loved and for those few days I forgot about his other life. The one I wished didn't exist. When we went out at home we took separate cars. I had to meet him at our destination and when we left, we took different routes but always ended up at the same place—my condo—to finish our evening. If we didn't have an event to attend, he rarely stayed past 8 p.m. He said he wanted to spend time with his children before they went to bed.

I'm always telling myself I can do better, but Oscar is everything I could want in a man. However, our situation has been far from ideal.

On holidays, I'm usually alone. On Christmas Day, there's a gift delivered to my home, but I have explicit instructions not to call him although I can send a text. I was also told that holidays, along with every Sunday, are for family so don't expect for him to spend them with me. The gifts were always so beautiful that they would temporarily ease my loneliness. The first Christmas I received a mink teddy bear wearing a collar that turned out to be a diamond bracelet with a diamond ring for a charm. But the gifts don't always compensate for the lack of Oscar's presence. When I'm at college functions and I see other girls cuddled up with their man in a corner, I wished I had someone too. I know Oscar would never go to a college function because of our age difference, and he certainly wouldn't kiss me in full view of everyone. We don't do public displays of affection. When we're in public, I am his protégé. As far as everyone is concerned, I'm some poor daughter of a crackhead he is showing some kindness to.

Once I started going out with a guy named Barry I met in my economics class just so I could have someone to hang out with. When Oscar found out, he was furious. He told me he was the only man I was allowed to spend time with, and if he ever found out I was sleeping with someone else he would kill me. At first, I thought his jealous rage was kind of cute and the fact that he cared enough to get mad over a college boy was funny. It meant he cared. I laughed, but that seemed to anger him even more. He took my new Louis Vuitton purse out on the balcony and tossed it down to the busy street below.

"That purse, this condo, your car, and you all belong to me. Don't forget who pays the bills," Oscar shouted. "Do you understand me? *You belong to me!*"

I screamed as my purse plummeted to the busy street below. I watched in horror as several cars drove over it. I ran as quickly as I could to retrieve it, but I live on the fifteenth floor and by the time I took the elevator down and stopped traffic to get it, my beautiful new purse was ruined and all of its contents, which included my cell phone, were smashed to oblivion. When I came back upstairs I was so upset I ran to my bedroom, locked the door, and cried until I heard Oscar leave. He must have felt bad because when I woke up the next morning, there was a new purse with a matching wallet, a

Nordstrom's credit card, and a new phone lying on my living room couch.

When I got to class that day I told Barry I couldn't see him anymore. No other man was worth that kind of drama. Barry didn't even ask why. I knew that he really liked me. He looked at me with disappointment, moved to another desk located three rows behind me, and never spoke to me again.

That was years ago. It still gets lonely sometimes, but we have to make sacrifices for love, right? I'm 21 now and getting ready to graduate with a BA in business finance. All those summers in summer school helped put me ahead of most of my peers. I can hardly believe I've been Oscar's mistress for 3 years, and he's kept his word. He still takes excellent care of me, but I've decided that I can't continue to be his dirty little secret anymore. I'll be graduating in 2 weeks and I've already landed a great-paying job at Promises Bank. I have been interning there for the past 6 months, and they are very impressed with my work. With my new salary, I won't need Oscar's money.

I owe my decision to make a change for the better to my best friend Vanessa. She attends a church that's full of people our age. She invited me to morning worship service one Sunday, and I enjoyed it so much that I started attending regularly. Last month was Young Adult Worship Week and on the last night we had a guest preacher from Memphis, Tennessee, named Marcus Jackson. He was tall, handsome, and spoke with such conviction. He began talking about how as young Christians we were called to live a life of holiness. That meant abstaining from sex until marriage. He told us how God ordained sex for marriage and the world has twisted it into something meant for our sinful pleasure, whenever, however, or wherever we want it.

I sat there listening intently to his words, but after a few minutes, I felt as if he was speaking directly to me.

"Sisters, I know it gets hard sometimes," said Pastor Jackson. "I know it seems like there is a shortage of good eligible bachelors and somebody else's boyfriend or husband seems like a good way to chase those single lonely blues away, but hold out for the one God has predestined for you. God is not going to bless you with someone else's man. That fine brother with money, a nice car, and more game than a casino comes in your life and seems to make everything better, but he's just making things worse. You didn't get a good man if he's wearing a wedding band. You got a liar and a cheat. You deserve better.

"When you go to the bathroom, you don't want to use a toilet that has been dirtied by someone else. When you open the door and you see urine and feces in the toilet bowl, what do you do? You close the door to the stall and you move on to the next one. Well, that's what you're getting when you mess with someone else's husband—somebody else's disgusting mess. If he was all that, he would be focusing on his marriage instead of laying up with you. So when you are approached by a married man, I need you to do just what you do when you see a dirty stall in a restroom. Turn to your neighbor and say, 'Shut the door and move on to the next one.'"

The church congregation said in unison, "Shut the door and move on to the next one," before Pastor Jackson continued.

"There are some women in here right now messing with a married man and God's got a word for you. He hasn't forgotten you. He's got someone wonderful in store for you, but he's not going to send him your way because right now you stank. That's right, I said it! You stank! He heard your prayers, but you became impatient and tried to handle the problem yourself. Don't be misled. That married man is not your gift from God. He is a pawn of Satan to separate you from God. You need to start taking a whiff of yourself. You stank, and it's because you got a no-good low-down married man up under you. He's not going to leave his wife for you, and if he did, would you *really* want him. Don't you know the cheater's rule? If a man will cheat with you, he will cheat on you.

"Flush the toilet, get that stank off you, and let God bless you. It doesn't matter if you've been messing with him for 11 days or 11 years. It's never too late to change. Ask God to help you and watch things move in your favor, but be warned. If you choose to continue in sin, you *will* reap what you sow. You are fornicating, and you are coveting. The Bible says you shall not covet your neighbor's house, wife, or ass. Insert husband in place of wife. That man doesn't belong to you, and you are constantly enjoying what should belong only to his wife. God is not pleased, and I'm here to tell you that if you don't stop what you're doing it's going to be to your own detriment."

As he opened the doors of the church and completed the benediction, I felt as low as the floor because I knew he was right. I was living in a fantasy world, and I needed to wake up. I tried to leave so I could be alone and think, but Vanessa wouldn't let me.

After service the church was having a singles mixer, and she wanted to introduce me to someone. She was always trying to hook me up, even though I told her a million times I wasn't interested. She couldn't understand how I was fine being by myself because she had no knowledge of Oscar.

We walked into the church fellowship hall and standing next to the refreshment tables was a man with the cutest dimples I had ever seen. Vanessa introduced us and right away I knew I had met someone wonderful. His name was Alexander Crawford, and he was the youth and young adult minister at Christ Be the Rock Christian Church.

We talked for a while over a glass of punch, and then we exchanged numbers. Crawford, as everyone called him, recently graduated from McCormick Theological Seminary and had begun working full-time in ministry.

We struck up a conversation and by the end of the night I knew not only that he was handsome but he was smart, funny, and a joy to be around. We saw each other several more times, and I found myself having more fun with him than I ever had with Oscar, and there was no sex involved. For the first time in my life I was experiencing something wonderful with a man that I didn't have to hide from anyone—except Oscar.

I have been hiding our friendship from Oscar for a month now, but I know he suspects something. But I also have to hide Oscar from Crawford. Fortunately, Crawford is celibate, so he never wants to spend the night and he never asked me any questions when I told him I would prefer we spend time at his house opposed to mine. I couldn't take the chance that Oscar could stop by unannounced. I knew Crawford was developing feelings for me, but he took his time verbalizing them. I wondered if he would ever tell me how he really felt. Then, one night as he was dropping me off at home after seeing a movie he said he had something he wanted to discuss with me.

"Melanie, I've grown very fond of you, and I would like to take our friendship to the next level. I know there's something you're hiding from me and whatever it is, I don't care. What I do know is God placed you in my life for a reason, and I've realized over the last few months I want you to stay there. I was wondering if you would do me the honor of being my girlfriend because I would really like to be your man."

I wanted to say yes right then, but I knew I had to end it with Oscar first. I wanted to be free to love this man openly and honestly, something I'd never been able to do. He was a good man, and he deserved that. I asked Crawford to give me a week to tie up some loose ends. He agreed.

That was 3 days ago. I planned to end things with Oscar tonight, but I guess not since it's his wife's birthday. I know Oscar knows something is going on because we don't spend time together like we used to. I told him the bank gave me more responsibility so I have less time to devote to him. I can tell he's disappointed, but he said he wanted me to be successful so he's backed off a little bit, but he makes sure he gets his weekly dosage of sex.

The next day I tried to busy myself and keep my mind off the fact that I wasn't going to see Oscar that day. As I got ready to go to the library to study, my cell phone rang. A voice said, "May I speak to Melanie?"

The voice was vaguely familiar but I couldn't quite recall who it belonged to.

"Yes, this is Melanie," I said still trying to catch the voice.

"This is Vivian Pendleton."

"Oh, hi, Mrs. Pendleton. How are you? I haven't talked to you in ages. Is the law firm treating you well?"

"Busy as always. I know you never hear from me, darling, but I never stopped thinking about you. My husband keeps me updated on your progress. He told me how great you are with numbers and that you are doing an excellent job at the bank."

"Yes, ma'am, the people at Promises are treating me quite well, and they are impressed with my work."

"That's good, sweetheart. I am quite proud of you. Considering all of the challenges you have been faced with you should be proud of yourself too. I know I haven't been there for you much. My husband seems to have taken on all the responsibility of mentoring you himself, but I wanted to try to make amends and invite you to my birthday dinner tomorrow."

"You do? That's quite all right, Mrs. Pendleton. I admire you greatly, and I understand how important your work is to the community. I don't want to impose," I said.

"No imposition at all, and I will not take no for an answer, young lady. It is *my* birthday, and I will have everything exactly the way I want it."

She was being quite pushy, and I didn't quite know how to say no. Instead, I said, "Why, thank you, Mrs. Pendleton. I accept your invitation."

"Delightful and call me Vivian. You are no longer the child I met 3 years ago. You are a grown woman who is about to be out on her own in the world. The dinner is at Chez Maison restaurant at 8 p.m. Wear something gorgeous. You do have evening wear, don't you?"

I had several dresses that had been provided by her husband for our out-of-town excursions.

"Yes, Mrs. Pendleton. I mean Vivian."

"Wonderful. See you at 8 p.m."

She hung up the phone before I could say good-bye. I decided not to tell Oscar I was coming. I'd let it be a surprise.

I arrived at Chez Maison at exactly 7:55. Oscar and Vivian made their grand entrance at 8 p.m. His wife was breathtakingly beautiful. She is the epitome of poise and grace. I once read in the paper that during her career she tried over 300 cases and won almost all of them. The word around town was if Vivian Pendleton was representing you, the other guy was in big trouble.

The Pendletons rented out the entire restaurant. There must have been 200 people in that room, and I didn't hear one person say one bad thing about Vivian. She arranged for me to have a seat at the head table with the family. In her words, I was extended family and deserved to sit with them.

After everyone sang "Happy Birthday," Oscar stood and made a speech about his wife. He talked about how they met in high school and it was love at first sight. He praised her for being a dutiful wife, doting mother, and a skilled lawyer always in pursuit of justice. He thanked her for their two beautiful children she gave him. Then he serenaded her with Lionel Richie's "Three Times a Lady".

Everyone around me was smiling. A few women let tears escape from their eyes, but I was dying inside. It was sheer agony to watch him display affection for anyone but me. I tried to sit still and put on a happy face, but when he picked Vivian up in an embrace, and then planted a passionate kiss on her ruby red lips, I felt myself becoming lightheaded and short of breath. As others clapped I excused myself and retreated to the restroom.

I ran into the first stall and threw up. Once I successfully relieved my stomach of its contents I walked to the basin to splash cool water on my face. Before doing so, I stared in the mirror and watched hot tears stream down my face.

My behavior was deplorable. I knew I was wrong, but I continued to infiltrate their marriage so I could get an education and live a life of lavishness. I was one of the most envied girls on campus. I appeared to have everything I wanted and didn't have to lift a finger to get it. But being the other woman had taken its toll on me. My conscience and what was left of my morals wouldn't allow me to continue this way. I had to end it for myself, for his marriage, and for the new man in my life.

I never made it back to the party. I washed my face and ran to my car as fast as my feet would carry me. I got a text from Oscar about 30 minutes later.

OSCAR: ARE YOU ALL RIGHT?

ME: YES. A WAITER SPILLED SOMETHING ON MY DRESS. I TRIED TO GET IT OUT, BUT I COULDN'T. I DIDN'T WANT ANYONE TO SEE ME LIKE THAT SO I LEFT.

OSCAR: I'M SO SORRY TO HEAR THAT. DON'T WORRY. I'LL BUY YOU ANOTHER ONE. YOU LOOKED BEAUTIFUL TONIGHT. I LOVE YOU. SWEET DREAMS.

Love is such a conditional word. It's really subject to the interpretation of the person saying it and the person hearing it. Could he really love me? I stood and watched him by another woman's side pretending to be the doting husband. He barely even spoke to me. When they arrived, he and Vivian acknowledged me with a smile and a hug like all the other guests. Vivian complimented me on my dress and said that it was a pleasure to see me. Oscar told me to use the evening as an opportunity to mingle among the elite of Chicago and he'd check on me later. Later never came until I got that text.

I tried to get some sleep, but I tossed and turned with restless anguish. Around 3 a.m. I picked up the phone and called Vanessa.

"Van, I need you. I've been doing some horrible, horrible things. Do you think God can forgive me and help me make it right? I've been sleeping with a married man. I feel like such a slut."

Vanessa was so nonjudgmental. I expected her to chastise me, but she didn't. Instead, she told me how to relieve my anguish. "God can save anyone, even a woman who's been sleeping with a married man. Are you familiar with the story of the woman at the well?"

"No," I answered.

"I want you to read it. God wants to help you more than anyone in the world. He loves us so much He sacrificed his son for our sins, and because Jesus died on the cross we have salvation."

"I want peace, Vanessa. I want the love of a good man like Crawford. Will you help me? I know I have to end this thing, but I'm so afraid of the outcome. I've been doing wrong for so long that I forgot that it was wrong. It felt so right."

"That's a trick of the enemy, Mel," she said. "He blurs the lines between right and wrong. This allows sin to take root in our lives and rot our souls from the inside out like a termite-infested tree. We look good on the outside, but eventually we will become weak and rotten and unable to fulfill God's purpose for our lives.

"Ask God to help you, and He will, Mel. All you need to do is confess your sins, proclaim Jesus Christ as your Lord and Savior, and then live according to His will. Getting salvation is easy. It's living a Christian life that can be challenging, but, Mel, it's so worth it. I have joy like I've never known. I have a good Christian man who wants to marry me and begin a family. I was just offered a better-paying position at my job. People think I'm doing it big, but I have to correct them every time and say it's not me but God. Ask Him into your life, and He'll show you what to do. Do you have a Bible?"

"Yes," I answered.

"Good. I want you to turn to John 4:7–14 and read the story of the Samaritan woman at the well. Check your e-mail in 5 minutes. I am going to MP3 you a song, and I want you to play it as you read, okay? I love you, and it's going to be all right. I feel it in my spirit. Check your e-mail in a few minutes like I said."

I got up and washed my face. I looked a mess. My eyes were wet and swollen from tears, and my nose was running. I cleaned myself up and retrieved my Bible from my bookshelf. I rarely read it, which was evident from the way the pages made a crackling noise as I flipped through them. I used the smartphone Oscar gave me to access my e-mail account and open the song Van sent. I listened to a man I never heard of before named Marvin Sapp singing a song that penetrated my soul.

He saw the best in me
When everyone else around could only see the worst in me.

He said those words over, but it was the next few words that made me yearn for a deeper connection with my Creator.

He's mine and I'm His
It doesn't matter what I did
For He only sees me for who I am . . .

As the song played I read the story of the woman by the well who had, had five husbands and now she was living with another man who wasn't her husband. She was looked down upon, and each day she went to the well to get water at an unusual time to avoid others.

Jesus was sitting at the well while she was there and asked her for a drink. The woman was startled that a Jewish man would ask a woman such as her for a drink because she was Samaritan and Jews had nothing to do with Samaritans. But she did not refuse His request.

Jesus then said to her, "You do not know the gift of God. You do not know who asks you for water. If you did, you could ask me. I would give you living water. Everyone who drinks water from this well will need more water later. Whoever drinks my water will never need more. My water will be like a stream that gives eternal life."

The woman said to him, "Sir, you have nothing to draw water with, and the well is deep. Where do you get that living water? Are you greater than our father Jacob? He gave us the well and drank from it himself, as did his sons and his livestock."

Jesus said to her, "Everyone who drinks of this water will be thirsty again, but whoever drinks of the water that I will give him will never be thirsty again. The water that I will give him will become in him a spring of water welling up to eternal life."

The woman said to him, "Sir, give me this water, so that I will not be thirsty or have to come here to draw water."

When I finished reading I said a prayer. "God, please forgive me of my sins, set up shop in my heart, and help me to make things right. Lord, just like this Samaritan woman, I realize who you are and that I need you. I do not want to be Oscar's mistress anymore. I have been thirsty for so long and unaware of my thirstiness. Allow me to drink of your salvation. I believe that you are the one true living God and you sent your son Jesus to die on the cross for my sins. Draw me near you, Lord. I want to live a life that I don't have to be ashamed of. I want to be a Christian." I prayed so long and hard I fell asleep on the side of my bed.

When I awoke the next morning Vanessa was in my condo cooking us breakfast. I had given her a key a long time ago in case of emergencies. I walked into the kitchen smiling because I knew God heard my prayer and everything was going to be all right.

As soon as Vanessa saw me, she ran up to me, gave me a hug, and said, "Welcome to the kingdom, my sister, a brand-new life and a brand-new you."

Over breakfast I told her everything. I also told her I had made up my mind to end the affair. If I had to lose my home and car, then so be it. I knew the Lord would provide for all of my needs. She told me not to worry. God had my back.

Two days later Oscar and I were scheduled to meet at the symphony. Vivian was supposed to leave that morning to continue her birthday celebration with a girls-only getaway with a few of her closest friends. I decided the best time to tell him would be after the show.

We met at the theatre for the 7:30 p.m. performance. Everything seemed sweeter that night. The music was breathtaking. Each note seemed to hold a beauty I never heard before. Oscar remarked that I was beaming. And when he asked why, all I could say was the God I serve was shining His light on me. He looked puzzled but didn't respond. He wasn't used to hearing me talk about God. The only thing that didn't seem sweeter was him. I looked over at the man I used to worship and saw a tired, selfish, unhappy man who manipulated a young girl who had no one. I wasn't a little girl any longer. If he really loved me, he never would have placed me in this situation. Oscar knew he was wrong and had been making himself feel better by buying me gifts. Well, the gifts meant nothing now. All I wanted was my freedom.

On our way back to my condo we stopped and took a walk along the beach. I was a little concerned because we never do things like this when we're in the city. We're very discreet.

As we walked, I looked at the water and the other lovers walking arm in arm or hand in hand. Of course, our arrangement did not allow for such public displays of affection. We just walked slowly beside each other. There was an eerie silence between us. I was struggling to find the right words to initiate our breakup. Oscar spoke first.

"Melanie, when my wife told me she invited you I didn't know what to do, but I couldn't uninvite you. I know that must have been uncomfortable for you. I don't know what possessed her to do that. I promise it won't happen again."

"I know it won't," I replied. I knew what I was going to say would anger him, but I didn't care. Loving him was hurting me, and it was now or never. Just as I was about to tell him it was over, Vivian walked out in front of us.

"I *knew* you were the whore he was sleeping with," she snarled. It was obvious by her slurred speech and wobbly demeanor she had been drinking.

"Vivian, what are you doing here? I thought you left this morning. Why would you say such a thing? You know Melanie is my protégé."

"I told you that to make you think it was safe for you and your little sex kitten to come out and play. Do you truly expect me to believe that innocent friendship mess? I have had a private investigator following you for the past month. Then I did some investigating of my own. You have been screwing this crack baby for years. How dare you! I could take you to divorce court and leave you penniless, but that would be too easy. I've devised a better way to make you pay."

Vivian then reached into her coat pocket and pulled out a gun. "I've decided to kill the two of you. Divorce would be too good for you, sweetie. I want you to feel pain the way I felt it when I found out my husband of 25 years was cheating on me with the mangy mongrel we got off the street."

Oscar and I both grew very still. It was as if time froze. I was fixated on the gun in Vivian's hand. I had never seen one that close, and to make matters worse, it was pointed in *my* direction.

"Vivian, you're not thinking rationally. I'll leave her alone right now if you want. You don't have to do this," pleaded Oscar. "Baby, I love you. I only have her because I get lonely. You work so much. You're never around anymore, but I wouldn't trade you for her in a million years. Please don't do this! We can work it out!"

Vivian began walking toward us with the gun gripped tightly in her hands. "Do you honestly think I'd take you back? I can't stand to look at you! I'm your wife, you bastard. I gave you two beautiful children. How could you cheat on me with a child?" she screamed.

"I'm going to kill her first, but to show you I'm not completely heartless, I'm going to give you two the opportunity to say good-bye. Kiss her good-bye, Oscar."

"What? Viv . . . baby—" Oscar began to plead.

She shot at his foot. I couldn't tell if it was intentional or not.

"I said kiss her good-bye, you bastard, or I will shoot you first instead of her!"

Evidently, Oscar believed her. He grabbed me by my face. I still couldn't move. I couldn't believe that he was really going to do it. He was going to kiss me good-bye before his wife lodged a bullet in my body. Tears streamed down my cheeks and neck. The cold Chicago wind made them feel like ice. I shuddered. I wanted to scream, but the sound wouldn't form. All I could manage was a soft whimper. I wanted to run, but my feet felt like cinder blocks and I couldn't lift them. Oscar slowly pulled my face closer to his and as he moved me toward him Vivian moved toward us.

He whispered, "I'm sorry, baby," closed his eyes, and then pressed his lips against mine. As he did, I felt Vivian press the barrel of her gun against my head. Another whimper escaped my lips as my lover continued to press his lips against mine with his eyes closed. He was going to let his wife kill me. He wasn't even trying to stop her.

All these years I had been fooling myself. He didn't love me at all. My eyelids seemed to be the only part of me that would move, and I closed them to block out the dreadful sight of this heartless man. The barrel of the gun was cold. I prayed silently, "God, help me."

I suddenly heard someone yell, "Police! Drop your gun and put your hands in the air!"

"Not until I kill this wench!" Vivian yelled with the gun still pressed against my temple.

"Miss, I don't want to hurt you. Please drop your gun!" he yelled.

"No can do, Officer," she snarled.

Oscar yelled, "No!" and lunged at his wife. I heard one shot, and then another one. A burning pain went through my shoulder. I fell to the cold sand, and then everything went black.

The next time I opened my eyes, Crawford, Vanessa, Boosie, and his mother, my aunt Tangela, were standing over me. I realized right away that I was in the hospital.

"Hey, lil' cuz. I knew you'd come around sooner or later. How are you feeling?" said Boosie.

It took a minute for my eyes to adjust to the light so I could see clearly the people who were looking at me.

"My shoulder hurts," I said. My mouth felt dry and yucky. "Can I have some water, please?"

"Sure thing, baby girl," said Aunt Tangela. There was a pitcher and a cup next to my bed. She poured me some water and handed it to me. I tried to reach for it with my right hand and winced. It hurt like hell. Plus, my movement was restricted by the sling I wore, so I reached for the cup with my left arm. There was a little stiffness but no pain.

"What happened?" I asked.

"You got shot, Melanie, then you fell and hit your head. The impact knocked you out cold. You've been out for almost 24 hours. Oscar's wife shot you. Your picture's been in the paper and everything. You're famous, cuz," smiled Boosie.

"My picture . . . in the paper . . .for what? Boosie, what are you talking about? Why would my picture be in the paper?"

"On account of that crazy heifer who tried to kill you."

"Boosie, that's enough," said Aunt Tangela.

"How much do you remember, baby?" asked Crawford. That voice was music to my ears.

"I remember walking near the pier with Oscar and Vivian. Vivian had a gun pointed at my head, and I remember hearing the voice of a cop telling her to drop it, and after that, everything is all fuzzy."

"That cop saved your life," explained Vanessa. "He was an off-duty officer taking a stroll when he saw Vivian put a gun to your head. When she wouldn't put it down, he shot at her, but her husband jumped in front of her. As she was falling, her gun discharged and shot you in the shoulder."

"Are you serious?" I asked. "Was anybody else hurt?" The room grew silent, and I could see in their faces that someone had been.

"Oscar jumped in front of his wife to save her, and the police officer shot him instead. The papers reported that he is paralyzed from the waist down. His wife was arrested for attempted murder."

I began to cry. "Nooooo. This is all my fault. All my fault."

"No, it isn't," said Aunt Tangela. "You didn't make Vivian pull a gun on you, and you didn't make her refuse to put it down when the officer told her to. Baby, that woman was going to kill you."

Aunt Tangela came over and stroked my hair. "It could have been a lot worse, Melanie. We could be planning your funeral right now. God saved you."

I couldn't do anything but shake my head. If I had ended it with Oscar as I told myself to do many times before, it never would have come to this. Everyone continued to try to make me feel better, but I was inconsolable. I asked everyone to leave except Crawford, and I continued to cry. His presence made me feel better. This woman was in jail because I was sleeping with her husband. My actions threatened everything she held dear. Oscar and I drove her to this. Her husband, her family, her marriage, her untainted high-profile reputation were all in jeopardy because of us. I didn't put the gun in her hand, but I gave her a reason to use it.

Crawford was silent for a long time and watched me cry. When I reached for his hand he just stood there looking at me. I needed him to comfort me, and he was refusing to do so.

"Mel, tell me that it isn't true. Tell me you weren't having an affair with a married man. I don't want to believe the horrible things they wrote about you in the papers."

I slowly looked away from him and stared at the clock on the white wall in front of me.

"I don't know what the papers said, and right now, I don't want to know. But I can't tell you what you want to hear. I've been having sex with that married man for 3 years. But the night I got shot—" I was cut off by the sound of the door banging shut. I never got to tell Crawford that I was planning to leave Oscar so I could be with him because he was gone.

Later in the day, the police came to see me. A nice female officer named Laura Green took down my account of what happened and asked me if I would be willing to take the stand to testify against Vivian if needed. I told her yes, but I hoped that I wouldn't have to be in that courtroom and give my side of things.

Thankfully, my injury was merely a flesh wound and my shoulder just needed time to heal. The next day I was released from the hospital, and I returned to class to finish school. It was almost time to take exams, and there was no way I was going to miss them and not graduate. I soon learned that no one saw me as the victim, but rather, a ruthless home wrecker who sought to break up one of Chicago's most beloved black couples. I received dirty looks from my classmates as well as my professors, but they were the least of my concerns.

My superiors at Promises Bank were unsympathetic as well. They rescinded my job offer and terminated my employment for unbecoming conduct. I was told my working there would be a bad reflection on the company. I studied hard to take my mind off the soap operaesque drama in my life. I passed my exams with nothing less than a B on any of them. At least something was going right. I would graduate magna cum laude, but I decided not to take part in my graduation ceremony. I knew cameras would be everywhere, and I didn't feel like the hoopla.

I was contacted by several reporters who hoped to get an exclusive interview from me before the trial, but I refused. They were the ones slandering my name. Why would I want to talk to them?

Yet, nothing I read hurt me as much as the fact that Crawford would have nothing to do with me. He wouldn't answer my phone calls or texts, and when I showed up at his apartment, he refused to buzz me into the complex. He wasn't the only person I hadn't heard from. Oscar hadn't tried to contact me either. I called to check on him, but the number to his cell phone no longer worked, and I was didn't dare call the house for fear that Vivian or one of the children would answer and say mean things to me. I often wondered how he was doing, but it was probably best that we didn't communicate. I didn't know what to say anyway.

The case went to trial 3 months later. The prosecutor wanted to wait until Oscar was well enough to take the stand. The bullet hit a nerve and several vertebrae and lodged itself in his back. It was in an inoperable position, and the doctors doubted he would ever walk again or be fully void of pain. A wheelchair and painkillers would now be ever present in his life.

On the day I was scheduled to testify, I walked into the courtroom and I saw Mr. and Mrs. Oscar Pendleton sitting in front of the judge holding hands. She wore a gray and maroon suit. Vivian had been out on bond for quite some time. Oscar wore a gray suit with a matching maroon tie. His wheelchair was parked at the end of the table set aside for the defendants. He had lost quite a bit of weight and looked very tired. His hair had more gray in it than I remembered.

He no longer looked like the tall, towering figure I fell in love with. I used to look at him as if he were Superman. The man of steel who could make all my dreams come true and all my problems disappear. Now, he looked like a mere mortal. His superpowers faded, and he was weak. This ordeal was his kryptonite. There he was in the courtroom united with his wife. I, his former lover, was cast aside like a stray puppy he found on the side of the road that he no longer wanted after the vet told him it was sick.

During the opening arguments, the district attorney painted Vivian as a cold-blooded killer who carefully plotted to kill her husband and his mistress.

The defense called Vivian a devoted wife and mother who snapped after finding out her high school sweetheart was having an affair. He contended that she suffered from temporary insanity and that the jury should have mercy on a brokenhearted woman.

The cop who shot her was called to the stand first. He recounted the evening's events and put special emphasis on what he called an angry, crazed woman who refused to put down her gun and expressed a ferocious appetite for revenge.

Next was Oscar. He looked so pitiful sitting in his wheelchair in front of the witness stand. His answers to the prosecution's questions were low and slow. I wondered if the bullet was affecting his mental capacity as well. He looked uncomfortable and lacked the confidence I was used to seeing him exude. Yet one thing was evident. He was going to stand by his wife. He professed his love for her and how he became lonely when she started working all the time and jealous when her career began to surpass his. I almost felt sorry for him. He told how he had sought comfort in my arms and gave minimal details about our time together. When his lawyer tried to attack my character I saw the spirited man I used to know. His voice grew loud and his words were forceful.

"Don't you dare drag that young lady's name through the mud for the sake of this case. Melanie Anderson is a sweet girl with a bright future. If anyone is to blame here, it's me. I took a young lady with low self-esteem and a bad self-image, gave her the finer things, and turned her into my personal naïve mistress. I even thought I loved her for a while. I see now I loved the way she made me feel. When I was with her, I was able to forget my problems at home. I used her, but I'm paying for it now," he said while patting the armrests of his wheelchair.

"The doctors say I will never walk again. I'm the one who should be on trial, not my wife. My actions almost got two women I care for killed. Yes, my wife pulled a gun on me and Melanie, and yes, she threatened to kill us, but I drove her to it. My wife is a remarkable woman, and I'm lucky that she has decided to take me back regardless of the outcome in this court. I want to make a public apology to her and Melanie. I was selfish and began an inappropriate relationship with a college student. I love you, Vivian. You are my first and only love, and when I realized that the cop was going to shoot you, I couldn't let that happen. I realized at that moment you are the only woman I wanted and needed."

Vivian sat there with tears streaming down her face. Her lawyer handed her a tissue. The bailiff began handing members of the jury tissues.

"Melanie, I'm sorry, sweetheart. I never meant to hurt you. You are a beautiful, intelligent young lady with a bright future. I hope I haven't ruined you. You'll find love again, and you deserve it more than anyone I know."

The defense waived their right to cross-examine the witness. The judge then banged her gavel and announced we were going to have a 1-hour recess for lunch.

As I sat in the cafeteria, the prosecutor came over and sat in front of me and said, "Melanie, I'm going to need your help to put Vivian away. She should be punished for what she did to you."

"Don't worry. I've got something for Ms. Vivian. She'll be so messed up that she won't know what to say when she takes the stand," I said.

"I was hoping you would say that." He smiled at me, patted me on the shoulder, and then walked away.

When we returned to the courtroom it was my turn to testify. I took my seat near the judge, and the defense began asking me questions.

"Ms. Anderson, were you having an affair with Mr. Oscar Pendleton?"

"Yes, sir," I replied.

"And how long had that affair been going on when you were shot."

"Three years."

"How did the two of you meet?"

"We met in the park when I was living in a homeless shelter. He and his wife showed me kindness and began having me as a frequent guest to their home. They even helped me get a scholarship for college."

"How old were you when you started having sex with Mr. Pendleton?"

"I was about to turn 19."

"How old are you now?"

"I'm 21."

"So from the age of 18 until now, you engaged in sex with a man you knew was married?"

"Yes, sir."

"What type of things did he buy you?"

"He paid for my condo and the associated bills like water, utilities, phone, etc. He bought me a BMW, and he paid any college expenses that weren't covered by my partial scholarship and financial aid."

"Were there expensive gifts, trips, and things of that nature?"

"Yes, sir."

"And where was Mrs. Pendleton?"

"I don't really know, but I assumed she was working. I know she worked a lot."

"Did you ever feel bad about sleeping with Mr. Pendleton?"

"At times."

"Why didn't you stop?"

"Because I loved Oscar."

"I'm sure you loved the life he was giving you too. There was no way you could afford those things on your own. Were you with him for his money? Do you think you're a gold digger?"

"Objection, Your Honor!" shouted Oscar.

"Mr. Pendleton, Attorney Payne is your wife's lawyer. He's trying to help you," said the judge. "You're objecting to statements by your own lawyer?"

"I know, Your Honor, but we're paying him and I told him I would not tolerate him damaging Melanie's reputation any more than it already has been. She is not the one on trial here!"

"It's okay, Oscar, I got this," I said. "Look here, sir, I was a poor black kid who got kicked out of her house the day after she graduated from high school because she wouldn't give her mother money to buy drugs. Then a few weeks later, my mother died of an overdose, and before she died, she gave the house my Grams left us to her dope dealer for a hit. I had nothing, not even a place to lay my head. I was living in a shelter when the Pendletons befriended me, but Mrs. Pendleton was always busy, so I spent the majority of my time with Oscar. He was my friend, and then our friendship escalated into something very inappropriate. I never cared about his money. I never asked him to buy me things. He just did it. But the most valuable gift he gave me was his presence. He was there when I needed someone, emotionally, mentally, and physically. I believe giving me expensive gifts made him feel better about the selfishness he was exhibiting by repeatedly bedding a woman he knew could never entirely have him. His guilt subsided when he saw me happy. You wish to paint me as a gold digger and a home wrecker. I was genuinely in love with Oscar, do you understand me?" I shouted.

"Calm down, Ms. Alexander. I understand. I have one more question for you. Do you still love him?"

I paused to think about the question. For the past 3 years I was Oscar's mistress. There were some wonderful times together, but there was also a lot of pain that I refused to acknowledge because I didn't want to lose him.

"Ms. Alexander, will you please answer the question," the attorney urged.

"Yes, I guess I do," I began. "But our time away from each other has helped me to see him for the selfish man with low self-esteem he is. Oscar needs a doting woman to validate him, and when his wife began paying more attention to her job than him, he sought that validation from me." I shifted my gaze from the defense attorney to across the room where Oscar and Vivian were sitting.

"You're sorry, Oscar? Well, I'm sorry too, but I owe the biggest apology to the missus. I am terribly sorry. I totally disrespected your marriage. I never sought to have an affair with your husband, but he was so good to me, better than anyone had been before. I never had anything as a child. My mother sold everything we owned to get her next high. Oscar showered me with affection and gifts, and I got caught up.

"If I were in your shoes, I probably would have tried to kill me too. I'm so ashamed of my behavior. I've asked God for forgiveness, and now I'm asking for it from you. The prosecution wants me to get up here and give a horrible account of what happened so they can put you away, but I won't. Ms. Vivian is everything I want to be: intelligent, beautiful, successful. When she walks into a room she commands attention. I noticed it from the minute I met her."

I turned toward the jury. "Ladies and gentlemen of the jury, I beg you to let this woman go. Put yourself in her shoes and think about what you would have done if you found out the love of your life was cheating on you with same young lady whose college education you were paying for. Wouldn't you want to kill someone?

"Look at Mr. Pendleton. He's already lost the use of his legs. Don't take his wife away too. It's obvious they still love each other, and they have two teenage children who need them both. I beg you to be merciful and let her go. Yes, she shot me, but my shoulder is healing well, and I'm expected to make a full recovery. Let her go home so she can continue to be the wonderful woman and attorney she was ordained by God to be. She doesn't deserve to go to jail. Please let her go. I'm sorry, Ms. Vivian. I'm so sorry. Please forgive me."

I then broke into a fit of tears. Instead of a 21-year-old woman, I felt like a 2-year-old who had wronged her parents. The judge told me I could step down, but I couldn't move. All I could do was cry. I heard people all around the courtroom crying with me.

Vivian slowly rose from behind the table where she, Oscar, and her attorney sat and walked up to the stand where I sat sobbing hysterically. She wrapped her arms around me and pulled me close. I hadn't been held like this by a woman in years. She wasn't my mother, but at that moment, she unselfishly served as my surrogate and allowed me to purge my sorrow through tears.

Vivian stroked my head and whispered in my ear, "There, there, child. I forgive you. It's going to be all right. This isn't all your fault. Oscar was wrong for using you, and I was wrong for ignoring our marital problems. I practically pushed him in your direction. Whatever happens, I'm going to be fine, and so are you. You are resilient, and you will survive. This isn't the end for either of us."

I heard her lawyer ask the judge for a brief recess. The district attorney never got a chance to question me. I was in no shape to continue. The judge agreed. He banged his gavel and agreed to a 1-hour recess. He then let Vivian escort me back to his chambers where I continued to cry. She rocked me back and forth in her bosom like my Grams used to do while I purged my pain and my shame. I knew the woman I admired had forgiven me. I silently thanked God for this miracle. I was afraid she would hate me forever.

Eventually, I stopped crying, and the judge came back into his chambers and informed us that court was adjourned for the rest of the day. I was also told that I wouldn't have to come back tomorrow. The prosecution decided not to cross-examine me.

Vivian and I said our good-byes. I knew I probably wouldn't see her or Oscar for a very long time, but that was fine with me. I exited the building and made my way to the street to hail a cab. I no longer had a car because the BMW was repossessed earlier in the week. Oscar was gone and so was my unlimited access to his funds.

As I approached the curb, I noticed that Crawford was leaning against the hood of his car waiting for me. He looked so handsome in his red sweater and khaki pants. My heart leapt for joy. I wanted to run over and throw my arms around him, but I kept my composure and slowly walked up to him. I hadn't seen him since he stormed out of the hospital, but I understood his reasons. Why would he want somebody's former mistress as a girlfriend?

"Hello, Mel," he said.

I smiled sheepishly and said hello. I knew I must have looked a mess with swollen eyes and smeared makeup. I was still clutching a wet tissue in my hand. I stood there patiently waiting for him to say something else.

"I was in court today. I heard your testimony. That was a brave thing you did."

"It was the least I could do. I could point fingers and lay blame, but I think all of us have suffered enough."

"I guess Oscar was that loose end you had to tie up, huh?" He looked down at his shoes as he spoke.

"Yeah, funny thing is the night Vivian found out was the night I was going to end it so I could be with you," I said.

He looked up at me and grinned. "Really?"

"Yes, Crawford, really. Why do you sound so surprised? I wanted to be with you. I wanted a relationship I didn't have to be ashamed of, and I wanted to start it off the right way with no attachments to anyone else. I was even going to tell you everything once I broke it off."

Crawford continued to grin at me. "You do know that I wouldn't have been able to give you what Oscar did. I'm not broke, but I'm nowhere near rich."

"I knew that, and I didn't care, and I still don't. Money can't buy love or sustain it. I want a man who is free to love me in full display of everyone."

He stepped closer to me and took both of my hands in his. "I came to tell you that I'm that man, and my offer still stands . . . if you'll have me."

I almost choked on my own spit. "If I'll have you? Why on earth would you want me? I've been labeled the biggest whore in Chicago, and you, a man of God, want me by your side?!" I said stunned.

"I noticed something special about you the moment I saw you. As I got to know you, I realized that you had a good heart. I've prayed about it, and God answered my prayer. These past few months without you have been torture. I have a longing for you that tugs at me morning, noon, and night. My friends and even my family think I'm crazy for loving you the way I do. They're afraid you might hurt me. But most of all, they don't want people talking about me for being with a woman the papers have painted as unrespectable. I told them, and now I'm telling you, I don't care what other people say. You're the woman I'm supposed to be with, and the good Lord told me so."

I laughed and said, "Who am I to argue with the Lord? It would be my honor to be your girlfriend."

Crawford then leaned over and kissed me outside the courthouse. I didn't dare pull away. I savored every moment of it. For the first time in my adult life, a man was kissing me in full display of everyone. That was the first of many displays of public affection between the two of us. It's something I cherish greatly because I never experienced it before.

The next day, the papers said Vivian Pendleton was declared not guilty of attempted murder by way of temporary insanity. However, she was ordered to seek psychiatric treatment. I thanked God. She didn't deserve to be locked up.

That night, Crawford took me out to dinner to celebrate our new relationship, and when we returned to my condo, there was an eviction notice on the door. I wondered what took them so long. The rent hadn't been paid since I got out of the hospital. I couldn't afford the place so I would have to move.

I'm homeless, jobless, and broke, but I don't care. I have God, a man who loves me, and a clear conscience. I realize that I have to pay the consequences for my actions. You truly do reap what you sow, but I know that just like Vivian said, everything's going to be all right. I serve a God who can fix broken lives and supply all my needs.

THANK YOU FOR READING THIS BOOK!

If you enjoyed Things Every Good Woman Should Know Volume 1, please leave a review on Amazon.com, Barnesandnoble.com, Goodreads.com or another review website. Be sure to tell others about it too.

Keep In Touch

Websites
www.jaehendersonauthor.com
www.imagoodwoman.com

Facebook Fan Page
www.facebook.com/imagoodwoman

Twitter
www.twitter.com/jae_henderson

YouTube
www.youtube.com/jaehenderson

Instagram
www.instagram.com/jaehendersonauthor

Blog: My Side of the Single Life
www.mysideofthesinglelife.com

Email
Imagoodwoman2@yahoo.com

Book Clubs
For the book club discussion guide, visit
http://jaehendersonauthor.com/book-clubs-xtras/

READ JAE HENDERSON'S OTHER BOOKS!

THE SOMEDAY TRILOGY

Available in paperback or ebook wherever fine books are sold.

About the Author

After embracing careers as a radio talk show host, marketing and media professional, and voice over artist, Jae Henderson decided to add inspirational author to her roles. She first displayed her witty way with words and keen insight into the human emotion through her inspirational romance trilogy: "Someday," "Someday, Too," and "Forever and a Day". She then released her first book of short stories, "Things Every Good Woman Should Know: Volume 1". Each book is a part of the I'm A Good Woman Literary Series, which Jae began to inspire women to accomplish their dreams while being the good women God created them to be. Jae is a graduate of The University of Memphis where she earned a BA in Communications and an MA in English. She is the former host and producer of "On Point," a once popular radio talk show geared toward youth and young adults. Other accomplishments include serving as a contributing writer for the award-winning, syndicated *Tom Joyner Morning Show* and using her chops to become a successful voice over artist. Her signature voice has been heard in hundreds of commercials and even a couple of cartoons. When Jae isn't writing, she works as a public relations specialist and college professor. She currently resides in her hometown of Memphis, TN. Visit her at www.jaehendersonauthor.com or www.imagoodwoman.com.

www.ingramcontent.com/pod-product-compliance
Lightning Source LLC
Chambersburg PA
CBHW071402170626
46811CB00003B/1225